Annie's Gift

Donald A. Shinn

Annie's Gift

Purkass Shina

Copyright © 2016 by Donald A. Shinn

All rights reserved.

Cover design by Donald A. Shinn
Book design by Donald A. Shinn

No part of this book may be reproduced in any form or by any electronic or mechanical means including information storage and retrieval systems, without permission in writing from the author. The only exception is by a reviewer, who may quote short excerpts in a review.

This book is a work of fiction. Names, characters, places, and incidents either are products of the author's imagination or are used fictitiously. Any resemblance to actual persons, living or dead, events, or locales is entirely coincidental.

Visit my blog at
http://donaldashinn.blogspot.com/

Acknowledgments

Special thanks go to my parents, friends, and family who have supported me through my struggles as a writer.

Thanks are also due to the members of the ABNA community for their support for writers.

More thanks go to my friends at the QVC forums, Vegas forums, and assorted other forums I frequent.

Table of Contents

Chapter One

Chapter Two

Chapter Three

Chapter Four

Chapter Five

Chapter Six

Chapter Seven

Chapter Eight

Chapter Nine

Chapter Ten

Chapter Eleven

Chapter Twelve

Chapter Thirteen

Chapter Fourteen

Chapter Fifteen

Author's notes.

Chapter One

"I'll get it," shouted Annie as the doorbell rang. She hurried to the door, looked through the peephole and saw their UPS man giving her a wave. She unlocked the door and swung it open.

"Hi, Marty. You're running late today. What have you got for us?"

"Not us, you," said the delivery man who was a regular at their home. "This package is addressed specifically to you, and you also have to sign for it."

"That's funny, I haven't ordered anything lately. What is it?"

"I don't know. I just deliver the packages and this is my last stop for today, so if you'll just sign for it, I'll be done and on my way."

Marty held out his tablet and stylus for Annie's electronic signature. She quickly scrawled her name then took the package and closed the door as the delivery man left.

"Hey Mom, did you order anything for me?" asked Annie.

"I haven't ordered anything for weeks," said her mother emerging from the bedroom where she'd been getting dressed to go out that evening. Annie's mother and her boyfriend David, though it seemed weird to Annie to call anyone that old a boyfriend, were going out to dinner and a movie.

"Well, someone sent something to me," said Annie setting the package down on the kitchen counter as she pulled open a drawer to get a knife to open the box. It could be a very belated sixteenth birthday present but her birthday was over a month ago now and she'd gotten gifts from everyone who would likely give her a gift.

"Who's it from?" asked her mother as she entered the kitchen while finishing inserting an earring.

"There's no name on the box, but the return address is a post office box number in Boston," said Annie as she slit open the tape sealing the top shut. "Whatever it is, it weighs a ton. Do we know anyone up in Massachusetts?"

"We used to have some family up that way, but we don't stay in touch. Let's see what's in the box."

Annie pulled open the top and peeled off some bubble wrap to find an envelope and a large book inside. She heard her mother gasp at seeing the book and then saw her take a step back.

"Is everything okay?" asked Annie.

"I don't want that in my house!" said her mother. "You've got to get rid of it!"

"What is it?"

"It was your grandmother's book and I don't want it in this house. You've got to get rid of it!"

"Who sent it anyway?" asked Annie as she opened the envelope and extracted the letter. It was from an attorney handling her grandmother's estate. Annie read the letter and was confused.

"This says my grandmother died two months ago and left me this book. You told me she died when I was a baby."

"She was dead to me even if her body was still alive. It was better for everyone that you never met her."

"What? Why? It's not like she could be worse than Uncle Mark."

"Your Uncle Mark is a drunken buffoon, but he's not really dangerous to anyone but himself. Your grandmother, now she's a different story."

"She was dangerous?"

"She was as mean, evil and dangerous a person as you'll ever meet. I didn't want her doing to you what she did to me. That's why I told you she'd died and we moved away from the area. She wouldn't have been happy I got pregnant and I didn't want her near you."

"What did she do to you?"

"Trust me, you don't want to know. I just want that book out of this house. Get rid of it."

Annie looked from her mother to the book and back to her mother again wondering what on Earth could be in the book that produced that type of reaction from her mother. One thing was for sure though, the first chance she got she'd take a look to find out. She just needed to buy some time.

"It's getting kind of late to get rid of it now. I'll get it out of here first thing tomorrow though."

"Okay, but I don't want that book here any longer than necessary. Don't open it or read it. Just leave it in the box and then get rid of it tomorrow. Sell it, burn it, throw it away, I don't care what happens to it, but get it out of this house. I've got to get ready to go. Dave's going to be here soon. Just leave that thing in the box, seal it up and get rid of it tomorrow."

"Okay," said Annie as she closed the lid on the box, pressed it shut and stepped away. "I'll be in my room playing some video games. Let me know when you're leaving." Annie turned and walked back to her room and waited. She heard her mother moving about the house then heard her mother's cell phone ring and eavesdropped as she chatted for a few seconds.

"Okay," said Annie's mother into her phone. "I'll be down as soon as I tell Annie."

Her mother stuck her head in Annie's bedroom door and said, "That was Dave. He's waiting out front. We should be back halfway early. If you need anything you've got my cell number."

"I'll be fine," assured Annie. "Have a good time."

Her mother paused and looked down at her again for a few seconds as though wanting to say something more, then decided against it. She said goodbye and left. Annie heard the front door close and then watched out the window as her mother joined Dave in the car. Annie was relieved to see the book wasn't tucked under her arm. After they drove off Annie hurried back to the kitchen and opened the box.

"So, what's so scary about you?" asked Annie as she gently lifted the book from the box and set it on the counter.

It was large, weighing nearly ten pounds, and covered in light colored leather that had been meticulously sewn on. Two large golden metal straps held it closed. There was no writing on the outside, but as she stared at the book she could almost make out traces of what had once been written there. Whatever had been written or drawn on the cover of the book had apparently faded or been erased as only bare traces could be discerned and they were barely visible.

"Let's see what's inside here then," said Annie. The straps took her a few seconds to figure out, but then by pressing down on the cover with one hand she was able to get enough play to unhook them. She opened the cover and was prepared for anything but what she found. Inside was page after page of nothing. The pages were all blank. She could see where there had once been writing or illustrations, but only the barest trace of the images was left. Whatever had been there had faded into obscurity.

"Crap!" muttered Annie. "I thought this was going to be good." After checking every page and trying to see if she could read even a bit of the faded out parts Annie finally gave up re-boxed the book, and left it on the counter. "Well, that was a lot of fuss over nothing."

The next morning her mother reminded her again that the book had to go.

"There's that used bookstore down the block," said Annie. "I'll see if he'll take it. Maybe I can get a couple of bucks for it. It's pretty if nothing else. Someone might like it for a decoration, craft project, or something."

"Fine, just get it out of the house. I don't want that book in my house."

Annie decided to try and get a bit more information. "So, what's in it anyway?"

"You don't want to know. You just need to get it out of the house. That book will bring us nothing but trouble."

"Okay then, I'll take it to the bookstore and see if I can get anything for it."

"Take whatever he offers and if he doesn't offer anything then throw it in the trash, but don't come back with it. We can't let that book stay in this house."

Chapter Two

Marcus Williams loved books. He'd always been fascinated by old books and had spent nearly all of his free money acquiring them. When he found out that one of the local rare and used bookstores he'd frequented in Philadelphia was closing, he'd cashed in his retirement savings to buy the shop and its stock.

He'd remodeled the bookstore to resemble one he'd loved while in college and over the last few years the shop had built a regular clientele that gave him enough income to survive, but getting wealthy would never happen. It didn't matter to him; he was doing what he loved and was surrounded by books. The only hard part was selling books that he loved and knowing he'd never have them again. His heart told him to keep them all, but his stomach and creditors told him that at least some of the books that came into the shop had to be sold.

Philadelphia was a great location for a rare and used book store. There were many older homes and estates in the area and most of them had libraries that were no longer in fashion. As the owners died off, those inheriting the estates were all too willing to liquidate the library and convert the spaces into media rooms, home theaters, family rooms, or other more modern uses. Marcus was more than happy to take the books off their hands. His personal collection had grown quite large and now exceeded five thousand books and rarely a week went by that more books weren't added to it. Books he had less personal interest in made it to the shop floor for sale.

An older couple was back perusing the shelves when he heard the bell over the front door tinkle. He turned to see a young woman carrying a large box enter his shop. She paused just inside the door, seemingly unsure if she should continue in or not.

Marcus flashed a warm smile and said, "Good morning. Can I help you?"

The girl hesitated for a second, looked back at the door as though considering taking off, but she then turned back to him, flashed a shy smile and approached the counter.

"I just got this yesterday and I'm not really sure if it's worth anything or not, but my mom wants me to get rid of it, so I thought I'd bring it here." She set the box atop the counter, opened it, and peeled back some bubble wrap. Marcus felt himself gasp.

He quickly reached under the counter and pulled up one of the precut pieces of butcher paper he kept there and then pulled out a pair of white cotton gloves. His eyes never left the book.

"May I remove it from the box?"

"Sure, but you don't have to be that careful. It's just a book."

"This is quite a book," said Marcus as his eyes took in the fine leather cover and the intricate metal straps binding the book shut. The style of the straps and the size and proportions of the book gave him the immediate impression that it dated to the late sixteen hundreds or early seventeen hundreds. He eased it from the box and set it down gently upon the butcher paper. Even through his gloves he could sense the suppleness of the leather.

"My god!" muttered Marcus. "Look at that stitching! It's remarkable."

"Uh, okay," said Annie. "I take it that's good?"

"It's remarkable. I've never seen hand-stitching done that well. Whoever made this certainly knew what they were doing. The stitching alone must have taken weeks to do that well."

"So it's worth something then?"

"What would you say if I offered you fifty dollars for it?"

"I'd say sold."

"You'd be a fool," said Marcus. "No offense intended, but this book is likely worth thousands and possibly tens of thousands of dollars, maybe even more. This is an amazing book. Where did you get it?"

"My grandmother left it to me in her will," said Annie producing the letter from the lawyer.

Marcus read the letter twice and then returned it.

"So, you're Anne Harvey?"

"That's me, though everyone calls me Annie."

"Hold onto that letter and the box, it clearly establishes the provenance of this book and absolves you of any allegation of theft, or inappropriate acquisition."

"Is it really that valuable? I find it hard to believe anyone would accuse me of stealing it."

"It's that valuable. I'm pretty comfortable saying it's the most valuable book in this whole shop right now and I've got some fairly valuable books in stock."

"Are you serious?"

"I'm being perfectly serious. This is a remarkable book."

"I should probably tell you there's nothing written inside of it."

"What?"

"Whatever was written inside is all gone. Apparently it faded out, was erased or something happened to it. Do you still think the book is all that valuable?"

"It's definitely worth thousands. Just as an example of a bookbinder's skill it's worth thousands. You've looked inside then?"

"Yeah, just don't tell my mom if you see her anytime. I wasn't supposed to open it, but I got curious. She built it up like there was something awesome inside, but there was nothing there. It was a major letdown."

"Would you mind if I opened it?"

"Knock yourself out. Just be prepared to see a whole lot of nothing."

Marcus examined the latches holding the book shut and felt once again that they were definitely from the seventeen hundreds at the latest. Unlike many of the latches from that era these appeared to be made from gold. Nearly all of the latches he'd seen from that time period were made of tin, or at most silver. To find a book with gold latches was extraordinary and their weight alone justified a price in the thousands.

He gently pressed down upon the cover and eased the latches open. He then opened the cover and marveled again at the quality of the construction. The paper inside was of as high a quality as he'd ever seen from that era and felt proper for the age of the book. He then methodically leafed through page after page and while there appeared to be some vague remnants of text or drawings inside, the pages were, as Annie had said, largely blank. He finally closed the book and refastened the latches and looked up to see the girl again. She had an amused smile on her face.

"I'm guessing you like this book then?"

"Annie, can I call you Annie?" She nodded and he continued. "This is easily the most remarkable book I've seen in the last twenty some years, very possibly in my entire career. It probably dates back to the seventeen hundreds, maybe a bit earlier. These clasps appear to be gold and from that era they'd be solid gold. A guess would be there are at least two to three ounces of it here which is worth thousands by itself. This is a very impressive book. Even with nothing inside of it I'd put the initial value at ten thousand dollars."

"Ten thousand real dollars in real money and not Monopoly money, bitcoins, or whatever?" asked Annie with more than a little shock in her voice.

"Ten thousand real dollars in real money, and there's a likelihood it's worth considerably more. This is a truly remarkable book. The gold alone is worth thousands. A book of this quality from the time period it seems to be from is worth thousands more. I think I'm being pretty conservative at ten thousand dollars. If I were selling it in the shop right now, I'd probably put a retail price of at least fifteen thousand dollars on it."

"It would probably be more impressive if it actually had anything written inside of it. Why isn't there anything written inside?"

"I don't know. You can see where there had been, or could have been writing inside. There are vague traces of what had been there. It could be that whatever was written was later found to be unacceptable and was erased in some manner. I have no idea how you'd erase it and leave the pages so pristine. It could also have been a book that had been written in some form of invisible ink. If I was betting, I'd bet it was written in invisible ink and the ghost images we're seeing are the words and images bleeding through."

"Invisible ink? I thought you said this book was old. Isn't invisible ink something modern?"

"Invisible ink actually dates back to the first century and could even be older. This book is probably from the seventeen hundreds so invisible ink was definitely around then and in many forms. I've just never imagined anything this big written in it. Invisible ink was typically used for secret love letters, intelligence reports, secret orders for military operations, and things of that nature. I don't know of any other example of a large book written completely in invisible ink. It's very intriguing and adds to the value."

"So, if it's written in invisible ink can we see what's written?"

"If I can figure out how to activate it without destroying it, we should be able to read it. I've got to do some research on invisible inks from that era and see how they worked. Would you mind bringing this back tomorrow and I can tell you what I've found out then?"

"Could I just leave it here with you?" asked Annie. "My mom doesn't want it in the house. She's not a big fan of the book for some reason."

"I'd be honored to have it in my shop. I've got a safe in my office that's big enough to hold it and I'll keep it there for you. Let me figure out a receipt of some kind for it. I'll do some research, and with any luck we'll see what's written inside. Can you come back tomorrow?"

"I'm off all summer until school starts up again," said Annie. "What's a good time for me to show up?"

"Can you be here at ten when I open? Business starts off slowly here, so we shouldn't be distracted then."

Annie nodded her agreement.

"Come on, let's get this book in the safe and locked up until tomorrow. I've got security cameras here showing the office, front door, desk and interior of the store, so the book should be safe here. This old safe has been bolted here for nearly a century and to the best of my knowledge no one's ever broken into it."

Marcus led Annie back into the office and pulled open the heavy safe door. There was ample room in the safe for the book and the box it was in, even Annie could have probably crawled in with room to spare. Marcus placed the book in the safe, closed and locked the door then sat down at his computer and wrote a receipt for the book that he printed out, signed, and handed to Annie.

"You really think it's that valuable?" asked Annie once more after reading the receipt with an estimated value of ten thousand dollars printed on it.

"I do," said Marcus. "It's likely worth even more than that. It is an extraordinary example of the art of bookbinding and regardless of the content, to find a book of that era in that condition is nearly impossible. The straps alone are probably worth half of that total just in their metal weight. That's a very valuable book your grandmother left you. She must have thought highly of you."

"I guess so. I just wish I knew more about her."

"Apparently this book was important to her, so maybe there will be something in it that will help you connect to her in some way."

Chapter Three

Annie spent a largely sleepless night wondering what was in the book. She finally gave up on sleep and did some independent research on invisible ink and lost herself on the Internet reading everything she could find. To her amazement invisible ink had been around for most of recorded history and had been made from substances as diverse as urine, blood, and other body fluids along with other chemical preparations. Apparently she fell asleep somewhere in the research process as her mother shook her awake the next morning and Annie raised her head sleepily from the keyboard of her laptop. A quick look in the mirror showed the impression of the keyboard on her cheek.

"Great," muttered Annie rubbing the area until the impression was gone.

"What were you doing on the computer all night?" asked her mother.

"I was researching invisible ink. That guy in the bookstore thinks the book was written in invisible ink."

"I'm pretty sure it wasn't written in invisible ink," said her mother. "My mother used to read it to me and the writing and illustrations were there. I guess they just faded away."

"What was it about?" asked Annie a bit too anxiously.

"It was a bunch of nonsense," said her mother. "You don't want to know what it was about. Trust me on that. It'll only get you in trouble. What did he offer you for it?"

"He hasn't offered anything yet. We haven't agreed on a price. He thinks it might be worth thousands. He wrote ten thousand dollars down on the receipt as a likely value, but he thinks it could be worth more. I was ready to take fifty dollars for it, but he laughed and told me I'd be a fool to sell it for that. I'm going to head down there today and see if he can make the print appear. Once we know what it's about, we'll settle on a price. It looks like it'll be a substantial chunk of change anyway even if the print doesn't appear."

"At least it sounds like he's being more than fair with the price."

"Yeah, I think he's a good guy. He may be a little book crazy, you should have seen his eyes when he saw the book and the way he touched it, but other than that he seems pretty solid. I would have taken the fifty dollars and been happy, but he said it was worth a lot more, so he's not trying to rob me."

"Whatever you get goes in your college fund and not anywhere else, okay? Oh, and be careful around that guy. You never know about people."

"I think he's a good guy, but you don't have to worry. I can take care of myself. Oh, crap! I've got to get going. It's almost opening time for his store and I'm supposed to meet him then."

Annie arrived just as Marcus was walking up to the door. He had a large canvas bag that he handed her as he unlocked the door.

"What is all of this stuff?" asked Annie looking into the bag.

"Hopefully something in that bag will let us read what's in your book. I was up half the night researching everything I could find out about invisible inks from that era and if that's what's in the book then one of these might make it visible."

"Neat! I was doing the same. I had no idea there were so many invisible inks out there. A lot of what I found kind of grossed me out a bit. Who knew blood and urine could be used to make an invisible ink?"

"And don't forget they also used sweat, onion juice, garlic juice, vinegar, milk, lemon juice, and more. There are tons of options to sort through and eliminate to find out what was used and how to make it visible."

"I'm just hoping it wasn't anything too gross," said Annie. "I handled that book with my bare hands. I'd just as soon not find out they used urine or blood to make the ink. I washed my hands five times after reading that they used to use stuff like that. If I found out the book was written in something gross I may have to cut my hands off. By the way, my Mom doesn't think it was written in invisible ink. She remembers her mother reading it to her and she said there were illustrations too. She thinks whatever was written there just faded away."

"Your mother said there were illustrations?"

"Yeah, she could remember her mom reading to her from it."

"Did your mom say what the book was about?"

"My mom's not overly talkative about this book and mostly just wants it gone. I've pushed about as hard as I can, but I get nothing from her other than the need to get rid of the book. I don't think she's thrilled about us trying to make whatever was written there visible again."

"Since there were illustrations that were visible recently then this could have been sympathetic ink that was used."

"That would be one where you needed to add the reagent to make the ink visible. Do you think her mother used the reagent to make the writing visible?"

"It could be. You really did do your homework last night. That could make finding the proper reagent pretty time consuming as there are many possibilities."

"Wasn't there someone who used perfume as a reagent, a queen or someone who used that type of invisible ink to communicate with her secret suitor?"

"That's what some of the history books say. I'm not sure how much I believe them though. I would think that would take a pretty potent perfume. I'm not sure anyone would wear a perfume that potent."

"I take it you don't ride the subways much. Trust me on this; there are people who wear pretty potent perfumes. I'd have killed for a gas mask on some rides."

"Point taken," said Marcus. "But some of the more common reagents aren't all that good smelling. Who wants to go around reeking of ammonia?"

"It beats some of the other options and I suppose you could mask it with some other scent. So if my grandmother was using her perfume as the reagent then the printing would appear whenever she was around. That's kind of neat and it's a lot less gross than blood, sweat, or urine."

Marcus unlocked the door to the shop and held it open for Annie. He then turned on the light switches and led her back into the office. He looked over to his fax machine and saw that several faxes had come in.

"We may have more answers among the faxes," said Marcus. "I sent out word about the book to colleagues and historians from the era and it looks like a few of them have responded. Chances are I've got a few e-mails back about it also."

He divided the faxes in half and gave half to Annie to look through while he read the rest. They then exchanged the faxes with each other. Marcus also checked his e-mails but they added nothing.

"That's pretty much what I read online last night," said Annie. "There's nothing new here."

"I agree. Let's get the book out and see if anything works."

Annie stood back a respectful distance as Marcus spun the dial on the front of the safe. Then she heard the loud clunk of the bolts withdrawing and turned back to see her book still in the box wrapped in the butcher's paper sitting in the safe. He pulled on another pair of the white cotton gloves before removing the book and setting it on the desk in his office.

"We'll get started with something non-destructive first," said Marcus pulling a flashlight-like device out of the bag.

"A black light?" asked Annie.

"You've got it. If there was print here that faded then the black light should reveal it. It might even reveal some of the invisible ink options. If nothing shows up then it likely isn't a faded ink issue."

"I didn't get a lot of sleep last night wondering what was in here. I was thinking maybe no one ever got around to filling it in, but my Mom insisted it had all been printed and she remembered her mother reading it to her."

"How old is your mother?"

"You never ask a woman her age, you should know that. Suffice to say she's forty-something, but looks younger."

"So a book created over three hundred years ago was easily readable thirty or forty some years ago and faded into nothingness now? No. That's not how ink works. It has to be an invisible ink of some sort, most likely using a reagent. Her mother apparently knew the reagent and used it to make the writing appear."

"We just have to figure out what the reagent was."

"Whoever commissioned this book must have spent a fortune creating it, so it's hiding something they valued. We've just got to figure out what."

"I'm hoping it's a handbook of some sort with rules for a secret society or something really impressive. Something where only the leaders of the group know how to make the rules appear. That could be neat."

"The thing is it could be anything. The only way we'll know more is by making the writing reappear. Let's take a look with the black-light and see if anything shows."

The two stared at the cover as the black-light was shone over the surface, but nothing appeared. They then undid the latches and checked some of the inner pages, but nothing appeared.

"That's disappointing," said Annie.

"It would have been too easy. Nothing good ever comes easy. The good news is with nothing showing up on the black light, it tends to imply that the writing didn't fade or was erased. The black light would have shown that. That means the invisible ink option is still the most likely option."

"So, what do we try next?"

"Heat," said Marcus removing a hair dryer from his bag. "That works with many of the more common invisible ink formulas. In the old days they'd use the heat from a candle or fire to read the print. A hair dryer should give us the same results. Could you plug this in for me?"

Annie plugged in the hair dryer and the pair stared at the cover as the hot air wafted across it for several minutes with no results. Annie reached out and touched the cover and it was uncomfortably hot.

"Ouch!" muttered Annie shaking her hand. "I don't think heat will work, at least not on the cover."

"This book is going to make us tease out its secrets. It's going to make this an adventure.

Just how much of an adventure became clear over the next three hours as test after test revealed nothing. They ran through nearly all of the most likely reagents and other methods and came up with nothing other than a cluttered desk and a trash can full of discarded options.

"It's possible there's nothing there," said Marcus after one more failure.

"I think we're doing something though," said Annie staring at the cover. "Wasn't that line a curvy line before?"

"Yeah, I think it was. How did that happen?"

"I think it was also closer to the edge before. Maybe we made a different part of the writing appear?"

"But how would that have made the old part disappear?"

"You're asking me?"

"Sorry. I just don't quite understand what's going on."

"You know what," said Annie as she pulled out her smart phone. "Let's take some pictures of the cover and some of the inner pages with remnants of marks and then we can see if they change. They can't be changing on their own and something we're doing must be causing it. If we document it, maybe we can ultimately patch all the changes together and make sense of the whole thing."

The pair spent five minutes photographing pages with hints of the old writing then the tinkling of the bell over the front door signaling a customer arriving pulled Marcus away.

"I've got to head home for some lunch," said Annie as Marcus left to attend to the customer. "I'll come back as soon as I can and we'll see what happens."

"I'll try a few more things while you're gone and, if anything changes I'll let you know."

Annie hurried home, fixed a quick sandwich, checked the Internet for any more information she could rustle up on invisible ink while she ate then headed back to the shop. An old man with an ornate cane was being escorted in by Marcus when she arrived and she waited impatiently behind him. Apparently he was a regular as Marcus welcomed him warmly and advised him that there were a few titles that had come in that morning that might be of interest to him.

Annie bumped into the man while trying to sneak past him and apologized.

"That's quite all right my dear," said the old guy with a bit of a twinkle in his eye. "You're a bit younger than the normal clientele here. It's good to see a young person anxious to get into a bookstore. My grandchildren have to be dragged into a bookstore. If they can't download something they don't want it."

"E-books do weigh a lot less and take up no space," said Annie.

"Ah, but you miss so much! The feel of the paper between your fingers just can't be replaced by holding a cold metallic or plastic device. The comforting weight of the book nestled on your lap. The sound of the pages turning as you work your way through the book. There's nothing quite like it."

"There is something to the feel of a physical book," agreed Annie. "I kind of like them myself."

"In fact, she's helping me research an old book she came into possession of," said Marcus. "We're trying to sort out a few of its mysteries."

"Is it anything that I'd be interested in?"

"That's hard to say," said Marcus with a small smile. "There's probably nothing there that would interest you. It appears to have been created in the late sixteen hundreds to early seventeen hundreds. I'm afraid we can't read it just yet. It seems to have been written in some sort of invisible ink."

"I dare say no one was writing early twentieth century poetry in invisible ink in the sixteen hundreds," said the old man with a laugh.

"I'm afraid not," agreed Marcus.

"Did you have any luck with the other reagents?" asked Annie.

"Not yet," said Marcus. "The office is open, head on in if you'd like. I'll be along shortly."

Annie went into the office as Marcus showed the old guy a couple of books from under the counter that had come in with that morning's delivery. She walked around behind the desk and saw that the security camera feed was on the computer monitor. She watched Marcus and the old guy at the counter for a moment on the monitor and then looked down at the book and was amazed to see both writing and an illustration on the cover.

"What the . . ." muttered Annie.

The cover had large block letters and read "An Illustrated History of the New World." Small drawings around the letters showed an odd assortment of creatures and people. One that caught her eye was an illustration of a green witch pointing a scepter at a dragon that had its tail wrapped around a large group of people. She rubbed her fingers across the cover and marveled at the color and intensity of the printing. She then undid the latches and looked inside the book and every page was now filled in. She leafed through page after page, pausing to read a section here or there that caught her eye and then moving on to another. It was fascinating. She heard a noise outside the office and looked up to see Marcus walking around the counter to escort the old man out of the shop. She hurried to the office doorway and waited until he'd finished escorting the older man out of the shop with his purchases before speaking to him.

"How did you do it?" she asked Marcus after he'd turned back from the door.

"Do what?"

"You don't know? It's filled in! The whole book is filled in! Come on! You've got to see this! It's amazing!"

Marcus hurriedly followed Annie into the office and looked down anxiously only to see the book looking blank, as it had before.

"No, no, no," muttered Annie. "It was all filled in! I swear it! What the heck?"

"It looks the same to me," said Marcus as Annie frantically leafed through the pages looking for any traces of the writing remaining.

"I swear to God it was all filled in a few minutes ago. Every single page was there."

"Did you take a picture?"

"No, I just assumed it would stay there. What the heck is going on?"

"What was the book about? Could you tell?"

"It looked like some sort of fairy tale book. The title was 'An Illustrated History of the New World.' Inside there were illustrations and writing about a green witch and a beast, but I didn't really read much of it. There was also something about an elf. I swear it was all there and I'm not making this up, or going crazy. At least I don't think I'm going crazy. Oh, God! Tell me I'm not going crazy?"

"A green witch, an elf and a beast? I'd have loved to have seen it. What exactly happened?"

"I came in the office, saw you and the old guy on the security camera at the counter, I looked down and saw the book and it was all visible. Wait a minute! The security cameras! The one here in the office should have caught the change. Please, please, please God let it have caught the change. I don't want to be going insane."

"Let me in there for a minute," said Marcus taking a seat at the desk and pulling out the computer keyboard and mouse. After entering his password and a few mouse clicks he was ready. "Let's look at the footage."

The quad view from the four cameras in the shop was on the computer screen in the office and the pair stared as Marcus rewound the video back to when Annie had left the office for lunch and then hopped forward a few minutes at a time. The book could be seen on the desk unchanged. Then, just as Annie and the old man could be seen entering the shop, the image of the book started to change.

"There!" shouted Annie. "You can see it!"

"I'll be damned," muttered Marcus. "How did that happen?"

The resolution from the security camera wasn't good enough to read anything but it was clear that there was printing and images on the cover of the book and also on the interior pages as Annie leafed through them on the video. Then as she got up to talk to Marcus the images started to fade until the book looked as it did now.

"I don't know what happened," said Annie, "but boy am I glad you've got a security camera in the office. You do see it right? I'm not going crazy?"

"No, you're not going crazy. There was something there, but what made it appear?"

"Maybe it was a delayed reaction of some sort? Everything was sharp and clear and it looked like it could have been printed yesterday."

"What did we do to make it appear though, and why did it disappear?"

"You're asking me? I just walked in and found it. Maybe it's shy and will only show itself if no one's around?"

"How would that work though?"

"How does any of this work? I was gone for about a half hour, let's leave it alone for a half hour and see if anything changes."

"We can watch it from the security feed out front."

The two spent the next half hour watching the security feed of the office from behind the counter only to see nothing happen.

"Okay, so maybe it's not shyness," said Annie.

"That was a bit of a long shot," admitted Marcus. "We've got to figure this out. There's got to be a reason it suddenly appeared and then disappeared."

"On the security camera you can see it appearing as I came into the store behind that old guy. I'm pretty sure it wasn't anything I was doing. You were just behind the counter so it wasn't anything you were doing. Was there anything going on outside at the time? Maybe there was a truck going by containing something radioactive, or something?"

"There could have been but the images were there for several minutes and traffic would have moved on in less time than that. Let's look at the four camera feed again and see if we can figure this out."

After watching it two more times and seeing traffic flowing past the front door normally they pretty much ruled out traffic as a factor.

"What about the old guy?" asked Annie.

"Mr. Ripa? He's a regular here, and it's hard to imagine he'd have done anything to make it appear."

"Maybe it reacted to his cologne, some medicine he uses, something. Maybe he's had a CAT scan or something recently that left him radioactive. He's kind of the only real option we have left at this point. I don't know what else it would be. It showed up when he did and left when he left. Maybe he's the key. Maybe he's the reagent we need to make the printing appear."

"Well, we can find out tomorrow. He's coming back then to pick up a book that he's ordered. He's usually here right around one in the afternoon, so if he's the reagent, we should be able to find out then. Can you be here around one tomorrow?"

"Just try to stop me."

Chapter Four

Annie arrived at the bookstore early the next day and spent the morning browsing the shelves and pulling down an occasional book to look through while sneaking back into the office every few minutes to see if her book had changed. She'd brought a sandwich with her for lunch and while eating that at the counter she'd chatted with Marcus.

"I'm beginning to understand why my Mom didn't want this book in the house. You don't suppose it's designed to drive people crazy do you?"

"It would certainly explain a lot, but no, I'm pretty sure this is just written in some form of invisible ink that we don't understand how to expose just yet. I've got some more e-mails out to a few experts to see if they have any suggestions, but no one seems to have an answer."

"If I hadn't seen the text with my own eyes I'd have never believed it. It looked like it had just been written. The ink was as bright and sharp as it could be. It was perfect."

"It must be reagent based. We just have to figure out the reagent."

Marcus looked up and saw Mr. Ripa approaching the front door of the shop.

"Here he comes," said Marcus to Annie.

"I'll get the door for him," said Annie hurrying around the counter to the door.

"Good afternoon Mr. Ripa," said Annie as she held the door open for him.

"You're becoming almost as regular a visitor here as me," said Mr. Ripa with a smile. "It's nice to see a young person showing such an interest in books."

"May I ask what that cologne is you're wearing?"

"You can ask, but the truth is I'm not wearing any."

"Oh. How's your health been? Any CAT scans, x-rays or anything?"

"I'm healthy as a horse, knock on wood. What's the sudden interest in me for?"

"You wouldn't believe me if I told you. I'm not sure I believe it and I saw it. I'm just going to slip into the office for a minute."

"That's a strange young woman," said Mr. Ripa to Marcus as Annie disappeared into the office. "Did the book I order come in?"

"It came in this morning. I've got it behind the counter for you. Let me get it out. You can take a look at it and if it meets your approval we can settle on the price."

Marcus led the way to the counter and then reached under the counter to remove the book and also to catch a glimpse of the security camera feed. He gasped as he saw Annie leafing through the now revealed book and snapping photos of the pages with her smart phone.

"Is everything okay?"

"Yes" said Marcus as he placed the book on the counter for Mr. Ripa to inspect it. "I was just startled by something I saw on the monitor. Could you stay here for a minute while I check on something in the office?"

"I'm a little pressed for time today," said Mr. Ripa looking at a pocket watch he pulled from his vest pocket.

"It'll just be a minute," said Marcus as he hurried back to the office.

"It worked!" shouted Annie seeing Marcus entering the office. She flipped another page and took another photo of the page. Marcus hurried around the desk and stopped her from turning the page so he could read a bit of what was written.

"What the heck is this?" muttered Marcus.

"I have no idea, but it's pretty impressive. Quick, let's keep going and getting more pictures before it has a chance to disappear again."

"Okay," said Marcus as he backed away.

Annie flipped the page and quickly snapped another shot, then another, but then the book started to fade again.

"No, no, no!" muttered Annie. "I'm not done yet. Is he still here?"

The tinkle of the bell over the front door answered the question for them. Marcus and Annie ran out of the office, across the front of the store and out onto the sidewalk, but Mr. Ripa had disappeared into the crowd. They each ran down the block in different directions to try and find him, but he was gone. After several minutes they regrouped in front of the store.

"For an old guy he moves pretty quickly," said Annie as she returned to the office with Marcus. They'd been unable to catch up to him.

"Okay, so we know it's him, or something about him that triggers this, so we're making some progress here."

"Yeah, but we still don't know what it is that triggers it. I sniffed the heck out of him and all I could smell was a bit of wood smoke. You don't suppose that's the key?"

"I don't think so. I'm not even sure he'll know what's doing it. What kind of a reagent could he be using that would account for what we saw that only he uses?"

"Will he come back today?"

"I don't know. He left the book he'd ordered and he really wants it, so maybe. He said he was in a hurry and couldn't wait. I just assumed he'd wait a few minutes. Apparently I was wrong."

"Mind if I hang around to find out if he comes back?"

"No, I enjoy your company. Let's take a look at those photos you took and upload them to my computer. Maybe we can learn more from them."

Only a few of the photos were focused enough to be able to read the printing as Annie had been in too much of a hurry to get steady shots, but those few focused pages were telling the tale of a green witch who prevented a war and also referenced a battle with a dragon-like beast.

"What the heck is this?" asked Annie.

"An early fantasy novel perhaps," suggested Marcus. "The writing suggests this actually happened and reads almost like a history text, but we know this didn't happen. I'm guessing it was some kind of an experimental text from a writer who didn't want people to know he was experimenting with writing about witches, wizards, dragons and the like. Writing a book like this back then could have been very dangerous."

"I wish the rest of the images were clearer. What we've got is pretty tantalizing. I was in too much of a hurry to get good images."

"Let me e-mail a few of these off to some colleagues and see if they recognize the text or style of the writing. Nothing jumps out at me as to the origin, but maybe it will to one of them."

Within an hour the first reply came but it wasn't the expected one.

"What the heck?" muttered Marcus.

"What's wrong?"

"The first guy I sent the photos to just responded. He claims the images I sent only show the book with blank pages and no writing or images, but they're here on the reply he sent me."

"That's weird."

It became even weirder when over the next few minutes the others he'd sent the photos to replied in the same manner.

"They're still on my phone and the computer," said Annie after checking both. "Hang on. Let me e-mail the photo from your computer to my phone."

It took her several seconds to complete the task and then when she looked at the phone she said, "It's fine. Why are their e-mails coming up blank to them but showing up here?"

"E-mail me one of the photos from your phone," said Marcus.

Once again the e-mail arrived intact on his computer.

"Maybe it's the book somehow?" suggested Annie. "Let me head down the block a bit away from the book and then send me the same e-mail."

A few minutes later she ran back in holding up the e-mail showing the blank book only to see it slowly reveal as she neared the book.

"It's got to be the book," muttered Annie. "What the heck is this thing? How can it control what's seen in e-mails?"

"I don't know."

"Wait a minute!" said Annie. "Look at the book! It's becoming visible again! He must be near!" She ran from the office and almost collided with Mr. Ripa as he came in the front door.

"Am I glad to see you!" said Annie as she grabbed Mr. Ripa by the arm and started to lead him towards the office.

"Ooh, the inner sanctum," said Mr. Ripa as Annie led him into the office. "I've always wondered what Marcus kept back here."

"Mr. Ripa, am I glad to see you again," said Marcus.

"I'm flattered but a bit confused. I just came back to pick up the book I'd ordered. I'm sorry I had to leave earlier, but I only had a limited time free and when I peeked into the office earlier you two seemed quite engrossed in whatever it was you were doing, so rather than disturb you, I opted to come back later."

"I'll get the book for you before you leave. In fact I'll give it to you for free if you could indulge Annie and me for a minute or two. We'd appreciate it. What can you tell us about this?"

Marcus turned the closed book around to face Mr. Ripa who pulled a pair of glasses from his vest pocket and glanced at the cover.

"I'm afraid it's not really my taste," said Mr. Ripa. "As you know I'm more interested in poetry and the classics than fantasy."

"Have you seen it before?"

"No, but once again it's not really something I'd have any interest in. Why are you asking?"

"Okay," said Annie. "This is going to sound weird, and I mean really weird, but the only time the printing appears on this book is when you're nearby."

"What?" asked Mr. Ripa looking a bit confused. "What do you mean?"

"Look at this video," said Marcus playing the security video of the last few minutes before Mr. Ripa returned. "As you can see the book's cover is blank and then it slowly starts to appear as you near and then when you enter the shop it comes into sharp focus. We believe you're somehow making the text and words appear."

Mr. Ripa looked from the computer screen to the book and back several times as he processed the information before speaking.

"No, no, no, no! This can't be right. This can't be true." He looked quite pale and more than a little afraid. "I've heard the stories of these books, but it shouldn't exist. They should all be gone."

"The stories?" asked Annie. "What stories?"

"Where did you get this book?" demanded Mr. Ripa forcefully. "I need to know where you got this book!"

"It was my grandmother's," said Annie. "She left it to me in her will."

"I need this book! You must sell it to me! I can't leave here without it."

"I can't sell it just yet as we don't have a clue as to its value," said Marcus. "I'm guessing the value is pretty high though."

"Name any number you want, but I must have this book!"

"How about ten million dollars?" asked Annie jokingly.

"Sold!" said Mr. Ripa.

"Seriously?" asked Annie. "You have ten million dollars?"

"Not at this moment, but I can get it. I must have that book though. You have no idea how dangerous that book is. I'll pay you the money, but I must have that book."

"Dangerous?" asked Annie. "You're sounding a lot like my mom. She kept saying the book was dangerous."

"Your mother is a wise woman. You must give me that book. I'll get you whatever price you name, but I cannot leave here without it."

"I'm thinking we're going to need to see the money before the book leaves the store," said Annie putting a hand down on the book.

Mr. Ripa looked more than a little panicked now and stared from the one to the other and then back to the book. He looked towards the open safe door and then seemed to make a decision.

"I'll be back with the money as quickly as possible, probably within an hour but keep that book locked within the safe until I come back. You have no idea how dangerous it is for it to be out in the open like this. Lock it away!"

"You're getting ten million dollars in an hour?" asked Annie.

"You'll get your money, but I need to see that book locked up. Put it in the safe now and I'll be back as soon as I can."

"Seriously?" asked Annie.

"I'm serious. Put it in the safe and keep it there and I'll be back with your money as quickly as possible. You've got to lock it in the safe though."

"Okay," said Annie nodding to Marcus who picked up the book and slid it into the safe, then closed and locked the door.

Mr. Ripa waited until Marcus had locked the door and gave it a test pull to be sure it was locked, he then scampered out of the office and the bell over the front door signaled he'd left the shop.

"Well," said Annie. "That was weird. Do you think he's really coming back with ten million dollars?"

"It would surprise the heck out of me if he did," said Marcus.

"If he does, then fifty percent goes to you," said Annie. "I would have taken fifty dollars for it, so if I get five million I'll be more than happy. Now, let's get the book back out and see if the print faded again."

Marcus bent before the safe and entered the combination and then unlocked the door.

"What the hell?" he muttered. The book was gone.

"How?" muttered Annie staring at the blank space in the safe. "I saw you put it in there."

"I don't know. I did put it in there, right?"

"I saw you put it in there. I was standing right here. Let's look at the surveillance footage to be sure."

They rewound the footage and saw the book go into the safe and Marcus lock the door then Mr. Ripa walked away and out the front door.

"Wait!" shouted Annie. "Go back a few seconds and bring up the front door camera."

Marcus did so, and there was the answer as to where the book had gone. When Mr. Ripa turned to head down the street, the book was clearly tucked under his arm.

"How the heck did he do that?" asked Annie. "Is he a magician or something? Were we hypnotized? What the heck just happened?"

"I don't know," said a clearly befuddled Marcus. "That is the book right? We're not seeing things are we?"

"I don't know. I feel like someone's reached inside my head and scrambled my brain. This has been a very confusing day."

Marcus looked at his computer and cursed once more.

"What is it?" asked Annie.

"The photos showing the printing only show the blank book now."

Annie pulled out her phone and laughed.

"Mine too. Are you sure there's not a gas leak or something going on here? Is this all a hallucination?"

"I don't know."

"I guess I'm not getting the ten million dollars then?"

"I have no idea what's happening. Do we call the police and report the theft?"

"Oh yeah, that would go over well. Our invisible book was stolen out of a locked safe by a little old guy who was the only person who could make the words visible. He then erased all of the photos of the book from our phones and computers. Once they got done laughing their heads off, I'm sure they'd put out an APB for him."

"We have the surveillance camera footage," added Marcus.

"For now, but if he could make the book disappear from a locked safe and erase the photos from your computer and my phone, what makes you think that footage would survive? Who the heck is he anyway?"

"I don't know. I thought I knew him, but this is weird."

Annie hung around the store until it closed and then returned home to find her mother packing for her vacation with Dave which she would be leaving on the next morning.

"Did you get rid of that book?" asked her mother.

"Oh yeah," said Annie. "It's gone. Some old guy stole it from the store."

"Well, good riddance in my opinion. That book would have brought you nothing but trouble. What was the owner offering you for it?"

"He wasn't sure what it was worth, but the old guy who stole it offered me ten million dollars for it before he stole it."

"Someone offered ten million dollars for that book? Seriously?"

"He seemed serious, but apparently he was just trying to get us to lock it into the safe and he stole it from the safe somehow."

"He stole it from a locked safe?

"Yeah."

"Where were you?"

"As insane as it sounds, I was standing in front of the safe."

Annie's mother looked more than a little confused.

"An old guy got you to put the book into a safe and then stole the book from the safe while you were standing in front of it?" asked her mother incredulously.

"Something like that."

"How did he do that?"

"I have no idea."

"It must not have been all that good of a safe."

"Yeah, I guess. Anyway, the book's gone and you don't have to worry about it anymore. The bookstore owner will call me if the money shows up, but somehow I don't think it will. He's offered to see if his insurance will cover the theft, but that would be one weird discussion and I have a feeling they'd just laugh at the claim."

Her mother resumed packing while Annie watched and then closed the suitcase and set it down.

"Are you sure you don't mind me leaving you alone for a week?"

"Mom, everyone knows I'm the responsible one of the two of us. Everything here will be fine."

"You know to call Mrs. Johnson if you need anything?"

"She's like eighty and is more likely to need me than me need her, but I'll be fine. You don't have to worry."

"You're not going to have a wild party, or have a boy around while I'm gone?"

"Seriously?" asked Annie. "I'd have to like a boy enough to have one around and I only have like two friends in the world and they're both down to the shore for the summer, so there won't be a party. Just go, have a nice time on your vacation, and when you get home the house will be neater, cleaner, and in better shape than when you left. Nothing bad will happen. I'll watch some TV, play some video games and just take it easy while you're gone."

Chapter Five

Annie saw her mother off the next morning and had settled in front of the TV in her pajamas with a bowl of cereal when the phone rang. She let it go to the answering machine.

"Annie? It's Marcus down at the book store. Mr. Ripa came back and is here now. He says he needs to see you. If you're there, pick up the phone."

Annie lunged across the room to the phone and picked it up.

"He's there?" she shouted.

"Yeah, he was waiting out front when I opened."

"Does he have a wheelbarrow full of cash with him?"

"I'm afraid not."

"Pity. I'll be there in ten minutes. Don't let him get away."

Annie hurriedly dressed and then ran down the street to the bookstore. Marcus and Mr. Ripa were standing at the counter.

"What the hell were you doing stealing my book?" demanded Annie.

"I'm sorry my dear, but that book is too dangerous to leave loose. It had to be confiscated."

"And how the heck did you get it out of a locked safe?"

"You two are certainly full of questions today, but I just don't have the time to give you the answers you want right now. I'll explain everything when I get the chance, but now I need to take you both with me to the council where it'll all be explained to you."

"The council? The City Council?" asked Marcus.

"A different council," said Mr. Ripa. "But, time's a wasting and we must be going."

"I've got a business to run. I can't just close it without a good reason."

"She said you'd get half the money, so I would think five million dollars was a good reason," said Mr. Ripa. "The council will pay each of you the five million you're owed, but we must get going. The council is waiting."

"How do you know I told him that we'd split the ten million dollars?" asked Annie. "We agreed to split the cash after you'd left with the book."

The old guy smiled and replied, "I know of the deal. I can tell you everything once we get there, but now we must be going. Time waits for no man and our time is running out."

"Some council is going to give me five million dollars for that book?" asked Annie.

"Yes, but we must get there soon. They've got some questions they want to ask you and we must hurry. The council is not to be kept waiting."

"What the heck," muttered Annie. "It's not like I had any other plans for this morning. So, where's this council meeting?"

"It's just a few blocks from here. Marcus, are you coming?"

"I'd better not let her go alone. Let me lock up and I'll go along."

The three set off down the block a few minutes later with Mr. Ripa leading the way and setting a very fast pace through the city streets. His ability to elude them the other day was now apparent as they were gasping trying to keep up with him. He was a very spry old guy. Finally he slowed and waited for them at the corner of Elfreth's Alley.

While they paused to catch their breath a tour group went by with the tour operator reciting his rehearsed patter.

"Elfreth's Alley is the oldest continuously inhabited street in North America with the earliest homes being built in the early seventeen hundreds," rattled off the tour guide. "One of the more noted features of the homes are the busybody mirrors which allow the homeowners inside to observe the comings and goings of those outside on the street. Our first house on the tour is up at the far end, so follow me as we head there."

Once the tour group had moved on, Mr. Ripa gathered the two and led them partway down the block.

"Wait here," muttered Mr. Ripa as he gazed up at a pair of busybody mirrors mounted on two homes with a narrow alley between them.

"What are you looking for?" asked Annie standing alongside of him and gazing up into the mirrors which were apparently loosely attached as they swayed slightly in the wind.

"Any minute now," muttered Mr. Ripa.

"Now! Come at once!" shouted Mr. Ripa grabbing them each by the arm and dragging them into the narrow alley between the homes. Annie saw a brief flash of blue in one of the mirrors before being jerked away.

"Ow!" shouted Annie rubbing her arm where he'd grabbed it. "What the heck was that for?"

"I'm sorry," said Mr. Ripa, "but the timing is critical and there wasn't time to debate. Come we must go to see the council." He hurried out of the alley and Annie and Marcus looked at one another, shrugged, and followed. They'd just left the alley when they first noticed it. Both slowed and stopped to look around.

The houses were the same but something was different. The air had changed. The smell of wood smoke now wafted through the air and the diesel fumes one typically smelled were gone. A horse was now tied to a hitching post in front of one of the homes and it wasn't there a minute earlier. The city was quieter too. The normal background noise had disappeared.

Annie looked back towards the center of the city and gasped.

"What is it?" asked Marcus.

"The city's gone!"

Marcus turned around and sure enough, the city skyline had disappeared. In its place were more old homes like those on Elfreth's alley with smoke billowing from their chimneys.

"What the hell?"

"There's no time to explain now," said Mr. Ripa. "Time's a-wasting, we've got to meet with the council. Let's go. Follow me and try to stay inconspicuous. You two stick out like sore thumbs here."

Mr. Ripa set off at a brisk pace, and after a moment's hesitation Marcus and Annie followed along shouting questions at him nonstop.

"Was that a time machine of some sort? Where are we? When are we? Who are you? What the hell is going on?"

Those were among the many questions Mr. Ripa completely ignored as he led the pair through the city streets. They went past a blacksmith shop where a blacksmith could be heard pounding away somewhere inside. A candle shop held hundreds of tapers for sale. A potions shop held a variety of vials and bottles in the window for sale.

The few people they saw were all dressed as though it were the seventeen hundreds and shied away upon seeing them.

"Mortals? Here?" muttered one old woman as she hastily climbed up her steps and bolted her door upon seeing Marcus and Annie.

"We're nearly there now," said Mr. Ripa, as they came to the end of a block. In front of them was a large city square surrounded by grass with a large ornate building rising up in the middle of the square.

"Come, come," implored Mr. Ripa leading them towards the front steps of the building where two men who appeared to be guards were standing.

"Welcome back. Mr. Ripa," said one of the guards upon seeing him, then he froze and a look of terror flashed before his eyes as he saw Annie and Marcus trailing behind him. "Mortals? Here? What is this madness?"

"They've been called to appear before the council," said Mr. Ripa. "We must be allowed to enter."

"I can't do that," said the one guard as the other continued to stare in shock and horror at the sight of the two. "It's not allowed. You know that. They shouldn't be here."

"It's okay gentlemen," came a new voice as an attractive middle aged woman wearing a large formal gown emerged from the door of the building and started down the steps. "They're here on official business and will cause no trouble. Step aside and allow them to enter."

"Yes, Madame President," said the guards as they cautiously stepped aside giving Annie and Marcus a wide berth.

She led the three inside and into a small room inside the building where she motioned for them to take seats before saying, "I wasn't sure you'd be able to get them to come and see us Mr. Ripa. It was a job well done."

"It wasn't easy. I've never heard so many questions in my life."

"Allow me to introduce myself," said the woman. "I'm President Marie Collins of the Council. I'm betting you two have a million questions and feel like your heads are about to explode. We've got a few minutes while the council is in recess to try and address a few of your more pressing questions. I dare say we won't have enough time to answer all of them, but we can get a few out of the way. Who'd like to start?"

The two looked at each other and then Annie shrugged and asked an obvious question. "Where are we, and when are we there?"

"You're in Olde Philadelphia. It's our version of Philadelphia. It's a parallel version that was created centuries ago to serve as a refuge for our kind. As to when, I'm pleased to report it is the same time as when you left your Philadelphia. Time behaves identically on both sides of the portal. Most of us on this side have never felt the need to modernize our ways, so we look a bit behind the times to you, but the time is the same."

"That alley was a portal of some sort then?" asked Marcus.

"Indeed it was, but only at certain times and under certain conditions. You know of portals then?"

"Only what I've read in science fiction novels," replied Marcus. "I've never really been through one before."

"It's a pretty simple step though isn't it," said the woman. "You just walk through and you're here."

"Which is where exactly?" asked Annie. "I know you say it's still Philadelphia, but two places can't be in the same place at the same time. Can they?"

"It can be a challenging concept to comprehend, but in fact there are more dimensions than one typically thinks there are. We exist in one dimension of Philadelphia while you exist in another."

"My book?" asked Annie.

"It is here being examined to determine how exactly it works. I'm afraid nothing quite like it has been seen for several centuries and we need to understand how it works. That's part of why you're here, we need to know what you know of it."

A bell chimed in the distance and the woman rose and nodded to them.

"Come, the council is returning to session. Follow me."

The pair was led down the hall to the large meeting room with several tables and chairs facing a raised area with many large, comfortable chairs, some of which were already occupied by various men and women.

"You may sit in these chairs," said the woman to Marcus and Annie pointing to the two chairs facing the raised area.

They took their seats while those already seated in the raised area eyed them nervously. One older man seemed to sniff the air and then act disgusted by whatever it was he sniffed.

"Can I get you anything? Some water? Perhaps a snack?" asked the Council President.

"No, I guess not," said Annie.

"Mr. Ripa?" asked the woman. "Would you stay by our guests and if they need anything during the hearing see to it that they get it?"

"Certainly, Madame President," said Mr. Ripa obediently.

"You'll excuse me now as I must attend to my duties. We shall talk more later."

She left the pair and stood while a small man emerged carrying a robe that he slipped on her. She then took the center seat on the raised area and nodded to the guards who then closed the doors.

"Given the unique circumstances we face today I think we can bypass the normal rules and proceed directly to the cause of this meeting," said the President. She looked towards the other members of the Council who nodded in agreement. "Now Annie, is it all right if I call you Annie?"

"It's fine."

"Then Annie, could you explain to the council how you got the book Mr. Ripa confiscated?"

"It was left to me by my grandmother. I never met her and thought she'd died when I was a baby, but apparently she'd just recently died. The lawyer handling here estate sent it to me."

"You weren't close to one another?"

Annie explained that she'd thought her grandmother had died years earlier and was shocked to learn that she'd been alive until recently. She then detailed the delivery of the book and what had transpired since then.

"What was your grandmother's name?" asked the older man who had disliked their scent earlier.

"I believe the letter said it was Myrtle Harvey," said Annie.

"We do not know that name," groused the old man with a frown. "Was that her maiden name or her married name?"

"That was her married name," said Annie. "Her maiden name is on my Mom's birth certificate. I think it was Letts or something like that."

Those on the council exchanged knowing glances and a few huffs could be heard.

"One of the Letts," muttered the old guy with disdain. "It would figure to be one of them. I should have guessed that."

"Did you know her?" asked Annie.

"Indeed not!" replied the old guy as if even the thought of associating with her would have been intolerable.

"I'm afraid your ancestors have something of an unpleasant history here," said the council president. "They committed certain crimes against our society that forced us to ban them from our world and they were forced to live in yours. Your grandmother was most likely the descendant of one of our most reviled citizens, a man by the name of Henry Letts."

"Oh. What did he do?"

"You don't need to know that!" replied the old guy grumpily.

"Alfred," said the council president to the grumpy older man, "Annie is not our enemy and is merely curious as anyone in such a position would be."

She turned to face Annie, "As to your family, this world was created to be a safe haven for our kind where we would be free from persecution. As you've no doubt figured out, we're a bit different from you. We're what you would call witches or wizards, or the like. Names don't matter too much. We just have different gifts than your kind. We're not bad people though.

"Henry Letts was one of us. He also traveled freely between worlds. It was more common back then. Pretty much everyone here spent time in both worlds. There were people who lived in your world however who wished to destroy us. They'd learned that we'd created a safe realm and wished to know more.

"Henry Letts had developed a hatred of our kind for some reason. He betrayed our world and showed those hunting us where our portals were located. Those who came or went through the portals were captured, tortured and if they refused to cooperate and bring the hunters here, they were killed.

"Those hunting us used those they'd captured to bring them back through the portals and they attacked us. They nearly destroyed our community. Those few who survived were very lucky. Most who'd survived had been living among the mortals at the time instead of here in our community. Nearly everyone who was here was slaughtered. Men, women, and children, none were spared.

"Henry Letts allied himself with our enemies and used them to attack our community. Those who were on your side of the portal when this went down were next to be hunted. Henry knew where many of them lived and guided the enemy to them. The survivors soon figured out who was betraying them and fled back here for safety. They then sealed the portals trapping Henry Letts on the other side.

"The portals stayed sealed for many years and then were only reopened after Henry Letts was confirmed dead.

He'd been killed by those he'd allied himself with when he'd outlived his usefulness to them. Hundreds of our kind died and we've been rebuilding the community since then."

"Okay, so he was a bad guy. So, you're witches and wizards?"

"Your words more than ours, but we're different from typical humans. We know things you don't and can do things that you can't, but other than different capabilities we're not so dissimilar. Our similarities allow us to mingle freely, but our capabilities cause some to fear us and want us dead, or to exploit our capabilities. Because of that, our ancestors created this world where we can live freely and in peace."

"So why's my book so dangerous to you?"

"We used to live open lives mixed in among the normal human population. Our books were printed and read just like yours. Then when the persecution started, the simple possession of one of our books depicting our history and lives was proof enough of our guilt for execution. As you can imagine, most of the books from that time were destroyed. A few of our kind found a method to hide our writings. They made it so that the text could only be read by one of our kind who wished to unlock it. The book would appear to be blank, or have a conventional story from your world in it. In theory your book should appear blank to all who see it, including our kind, unless we demand it to reveal itself, but for some reason it becomes visible whenever in the presence of anyone from our world.

"Our researchers think it may be due to the time that's passed since the original owner of the book passed. His or her control of the book has weakened and now the book is viewable to anyone from our world. It no longer requires a conscious effort to unlock it and make the writing visible. Merely being in the presence of one of our kind is sufficient."

"So if my grandmother was like you, the book would have been readable to her and my mother?"

"Yes, in all likelihood. The book would have sensed her power and unlocked itself for her."

"You make it sound like the book is alive," said Annie.

"In some ways it is," said the President. "In some ways everything is alive. Now the danger from this book comes with it being unlocked by merely being in the presence of one of our kind. This could make it a valuable tool to be able to be used to detect us. There are still those who wish to hunt us down and either kill, or exploit us. With a book like this in their possession they could identify our kind and do as they wish with us.

"That book contains hundreds of pages and each page could be cut into segments and each segment given to a hunter of our kind. With hundreds, possibly thousands of such segments out there, anyone crossing into your world would be at great risk of being detected. Hunters could simply carry a segment of the book with them and whenever text appeared they would know they were in the presence of one of our kind. There have been instances of this before using certain relics from the time before we were hunted. We thought we'd found and confiscated all of them, but this book somehow escaped our detection."

"So the book would be bad if it fell into the wrong hands?"

"It could be used to capture any of our kind who ventures into your world, or to track them as they use the portals and then exploit the portals to come here and destroy us. As you've seen, mortals can use our portals when assisted by one of our kind. The potential danger was recognized by Mr. Ripa and that's why he confiscated your book. I understand you agreed on a selling price before he took it?"

"We did," said Annie. "I was mostly joking though."

"What price did you agree on?" asked the Council President.

"Ten million dollars," said Annie sheepishly.

"What?" bellowed the cranky older guy as Mr. Ripa slid behind Marcus and Annie to hide. "Ten million dollars?"

"A bargain at twice that price," said the Council President. "We will find a way to get the money to you. It likely won't come as a large cash sum, but we've got ways of getting the money to you."

"It's got to go in my college fund, so it's not like I'll be spending it soon anyway."

"You will get your money. I believe you two had agreed to split the funds?"

"That's not really necessary," said Marcus. "It would be hard for me to explain the sudden appearance of five million dollars in my bank account. The IRS would want an explanation and I'm not sure they'd believe me if I told them about this."

"I have a strong suspicion you'll soon find some interesting and valuable titles arriving at your bookstore complete with the proper invoices. It may take a few years to make it the full five million you're due, but you'll get your money's worth."

"Can I ask a weird question?" asked Annie.

"You may ask anything," said the Council President.

"Could I read the book? What little I read was fascinating and I'd love to know more. The photos I took were mostly blurry and impossible to read."

"The photos showed the printing?" asked a small man sitting at the end of the bench.

"They did while the book was there, but then they disappeared when the book did. Here, I'll show you."

Annie pulled out her smart phone and pulled up the photos and was surprised to see them back on the phone.

"Here they are. The book must be nearby as the images are there again." She handed her phone to the man who had come over to observe. He went rather pale as he leafed through the photos.

"Samuel?" asked the Council President. "Is something wrong?"

"This is bad! This is so, so bad!" muttered the man still holding the phone.

"It's not that bad. The printing is only there when the book is around," said Annie.

"That's just it," said Samuel. "The book isn't nearby. These images are reacting to us and not the book. This phone can be used to detect us. Did you send any of these images to anyone?"

"Yes," said Marcus. "I forwarded the images to some other book experts in a few e-mails."

"Samuel, are you saying that the e-mails are also a danger?" asked the Council President.

"I'll have to run some tests. But, I'm afraid it might be that way. I'll know more tomorrow. If true, then there could be endless copies of the messages circulated. This could be a far larger danger than we'd assumed."

"Well, that complicates matters a bit," said the Council President. "My friends, I'm afraid I'm going to have to ask you to stay here with us overnight while Samuel and his team examine this situation. There's a lovely inn just down the block where we can put you up for the night while Samuel looks into this matter. I'm afraid we don't have much choice here."

"I've got a business to run," said Marcus. "I can't just leave it."

"There's a bookstore here in town that will almost certainly have a number of titles you'd love to have for your store," said the Council President. "I'll see to it that you have your pick of any books in the store for your store as part of your compensation. Think of this as a book acquisition trip. And Annie, will your being here cause any issues with your mother?"

"No, she's on vacation and isn't home anyway so I won't be missed."

"Excellent, then Mr. Ripa will show you to the room where we initially talked and I'll come pick you up from there once council business has ended. It shouldn't take long to finish our business here today, but I suspect you three will have plenty to talk about while you wait. We'll get some books for your store, have a good supper and get you settled in at the inn. With any luck we can get everything squared away tomorrow morning and put this whole matter behind us."

Mr. Ripa led the two back to the original room and then disappeared for a few minutes before returning with some sandwiches and drinks for them.

"So, you're one of them?" asked Marcus.

"Indeed I am," said Mr. Ripa.

"And this is all real? It's not some elaborate prank, or drug induced state?"

"It's all real. Just wait until you get into Worm's bookstore. That may seem unreal to you."

"Why?" asked Marcus.

"He's got books in there that you can only dream of. He's got first edition Dickens, some Shakespeare drafts thought lost forever, and more. The only real issue is that most of his stuff is older and my taste runs to the newer works. That's why I shop in your store. But for you, Worm's bookstore will blow your mind."

"Just tell me he's not a real worm?"

"No, he's as normal appearing as the rest of us. There are some in our world who differ in appearance. You've read of the Green Witch in the book? She created the first sanctuary on this side because it's hard to blend in when you're green. When the first persecutions started she would have been too easy a target. Likewise Elf Reth created the first few streets here in Olde Philadelphia. As an elf he kind of stood out a bit in your world."

"Elf Reth?" asked Annie. "As in Elfreth's alley?"

"His name does kind of hide in plain sight, but so does the Green Witch. Her first sanctuary was a village in New York."

"Greenwich Village?" asked Marcus.

"Yes, we aren't as hidden as a lot of people think we are. You just have to know where to look. You can drop one of my kind pretty much anywhere in the world and based on the local names they can find a sanctuary. You just have to know what to look for."

"So, Elf Reth was a real guy?" asked Annie.

"He was a blacksmith," said Mr. Ripa. "And he was a good one too. Much of what he made is still in use here to this day He also possessed greater than normal abilities and was able to carve out the initial blocks of Olde Philadelphia. Since then it's grown a bit and expanded at other's hands, but he started this world."

"Why is this place so stuck in the past? I would think you guys would have flying cars and what not. Speaking of which, where are all of the flying brooms?"

"I'm afraid flying brooms are largely a myth. I'm sure some could make a flying broom if they wanted to, but there are easier ways to travel. As to being stuck in the past, well, this style of life suits our needs. We're happy here."

"Indeed we are," said the President of the Council as she swept into the room without her formal robe on.

Annie was a little surprised to find her wearing blue jeans and a comfy looking modern shirt.

"You look a lot more comfortable," said Annie.

"I'm not a big fan of formality and I do travel back and forth between worlds fairly frequently, so I've become used to your more modern attire. Now is probably a good time to hit that bookstore I told you about, and then we'll head to the inn to get some supper and set up your lodging for the night."

The President led them out into the street and she walked at a more leisurely pace allowing Annie and Marcus to take in more of the surroundings and ask her more questions.

"This is so weird," said Marcus. "It's really like we've gone back in a time machine."

"But it's still Philadelphia. Right now we're only a few hundred yards from your store," said the President. "It would be just over there."

Where she pointed was a large open field with a few cattle grazing in it.

"That's amazing!" muttered Marcus.

"They're called cows," said the President with a grin. "Come, we're almost to the bookstore."

Annie was surprised to see people still pulling away from them and disappearing.

"Why is everyone so afraid of us?" asked Annie.

"I'm afraid the only knowledge many here have of your world is from our past and the news brought back by those of us who travel back and forth, and there aren't that many of us who do so these days. Some like to make your world seem more dangerous than it really is. Here, we have a population of a little over three hundred. No one can remember the last time a major crime occurred. Everyone knows one another and there's mutual respect.

"When a newspaper from your Philadelphia comes across, those who don't travel back and forth read of the horrific crimes that have taken place in just twenty-four hours, and it makes your world appear enormously dangerous. It becomes easy to assume that everyone there must be a deranged killer. They lose sight of how many people there are in your Philadelphia and how small a percentage are criminals, or victims of crime. It colors their perception of mortals. They feel safe here, and seeing mortals here is disconcerting to them."

She paused in front of a store with a wooden sign showing a large bookworm wearing glasses peering out from a book.

"Here's the bookstore. Mr. Worm is a regular traveler between the worlds, so he should be comfortable in your presence."

"I just always thought that if I met a real witch or wizard, that I'd be the one scared of them and not the other way around," said Annie.

"Your fear is based on a preconceived notion of what witches and wizards are. You don't seem afraid of Mr. Ripa, or me however. We don't fit your preconception. If we were dressed in black and acting sinister, as portrayed in your films and books, you'd likely fear us. The fear those who only live here have is based on a preconceived notion of what your kind are, and there's lots of documentation showing the brutality of some of your kind. When was the last time you read of a witch or wizard harming someone in your world?"

"That would be never."

"But they read of the violence and crime in your world in every newspaper that crosses over. And they know of the horrors your kind committed when they came here earlier. It gives them a good reason to fear all mortals. Come, let's go inside and see if we can't find some books for the store."

For the next few hours Annie asked many more questions of the President while Marcus was shown book after book by Mr. Worm.

"So my book tells the real history of early America?"

"Indeed it does. History is written by the victors and I'm afraid our kind were not the victors, but the victims. Our accomplishments were wiped from your history and hidden from the mortal population. The Green witch, Elf Reth and many others played vital roles in the establishing of the country, but their roles are unknown on your side of the portal. What you know is but a fraction of what really happened."

A clock chimed in the distance and the president frowned.

"I'm afraid I'm going to have to interrupt the shopping trip and get us to the inn for some supper and to arrange lodging for you," said the President as Marcus stared adoringly at a first edition Dickens that had been produced.

"This place is amazing!" muttered Marcus. "I've only dreamed of seeing some of these books."

"Well," said the President. "As repayment for your services you will soon enough own some of them. Mr. Worm will arrange for their transport to your store. But for now, we've got to get to the inn."

The President led them through the streets until she paused outside an inn with the name "The Rooster Crows." She turned to face the two.

"I should warn you that the reception here might be a tick awkward. They aren't used to having people from your side of the portal here. Just follow my lead and all should be fine."

She then led them inside. As they came up the front steps they could see a woman standing behind a counter look out and see them. An expression of horror crossed her face and she quickly disappeared back into a room behind the front desk as they entered. To the right was a dining room with ten tables, eight of which had at least one patron sitting there eating dinner. A gasp came from one of the patrons upon seeing the trio and whispers and quickly turning heads soon had everyone in the room staring at them.

"There, there, now," said the President. "Everyone go back to what you were doing. There's no need to make my friends feel awkward."

"Friends?" came a murmur from a nearby table.

"Indeed. These are good friends of mine and our community who are here at the request of the Council. Our business has unexpectedly taken a turn that requires them to stay longer than initially expected, so I've brought them here for supper. Now, go back about your business."

Heads slowly turned back to their plates, but few in the room appeared comfortable.

The President led the pair to an empty table and smiled as the patrons at adjoining tables hurriedly gulped down their food and stood to leave. In minutes the dining room was empty except for the three of them.

"I should bring you two with me all of the time," said the President. "It's often hard to get a table here. Now if only we could get some service." The last line was said loudly and clearly intended to be overheard by the staff.

At the back of the room was a curtained off doorway and shuffling could be heard coming from there along with muted protests. Then a young woman was literally shoved out into the dining room. She quickly tried to retreat, but hidden hands behind the curtain pushed her back into the room.

"Ah," said the President with a smile. "Mary, isn't it? Would you mind taking our orders?"

The young woman looked past the table to the door leading out of the dining room and apparently briefly considered fleeing that way, but finally gave up that idea and slowly approached the table.

"What, what, what would you like?" asked the young woman nervously standing nearly ten feet away.

"You needn't be afraid of us," said Annie with a smile. "We're not a threat to you. We don't want to hurt anyone. We just want something to eat."

Her assurances only made Mary take an additional half step backwards away from the table.

"Is that beef stew I smell?" asked the President.

"Yes, Ma'am," said Mary nervously.

The President turned to the other two and said, "The beef stew here is excellent. May I recommend that and a loaf of their bread? The bread here is simply divine."

Annie and Marcus looked to one another and nodded their agreement.

"Excellent!" said the President. "We'd like three servings of the beef stew then and a loaf of your bread."

"Yes, Ma'am," said Mary just before turning her back and racing to the kitchen where she ducked under the curtain and disappeared.

"So," asked the President. "How are you enjoying your time here?"

"It's different," said Annie. "I've never had anyone deathly afraid of me before. That takes some getting used to."

"Indeed it does. You can imagine what it was like for our kind when we became feared. Many of us had been healers, advisers, and respected members of the communities in which we'd lived. Then fear took over, and we went from being a part of the community to outcasts, and eventually the hunted. Have no fear though; no one here will hunt you."

More noise could be heard coming from the kitchen and then Mary was shoved back out from behind the curtain. A tray was slid out under the curtain containing three bowls of beef stew and a large loaf of bread. Mary briefly tried to slide back through the curtain to no avail as hands pressed her into the dining room.

"It's okay, Mary," said the President calmly. "No harm will come to you. Just deliver the food."

"Yes, Ma'am," Mary said nervously. She put the tray between herself and the table and then bent down to lift it up without ever taking her eyes off the table. She very slowly walked towards the table and then stopped a table away and was clearly shaking with fear.

"Oh, for God's sake," muttered Annie. "We're not dangerous."

"They're friends Mary," said the President. "They will do you no harm."

"Yes, Ma'am," said Mary, but it was clear that she didn't believe a word of it.

"Look," said Annie. "Just leave the food at that table and I'll come get it once you feel like you're a safe distance away."

"That's not necessary, Annie," said the President. "Mary will be only too happy to serve us. Won't you Mary? It is her job after all."

"Yes, Ma'am," said Mary. She nervously shuffled forward a few more steps and then paused behind the President's chair and picked up one of the bowls of stew. Her hand was shaking so badly that ripples were appearing on the surface of the stew. The President took the girl's hand and guided it down to the table keeping the spilled stew to a minimum. Without letting go of Mary's hand she then guided it back to the tray to pick up a second bowl of stew which she guided towards Annie's spot at the table. Mary's hand shaking was now creating waves in the beef stew despite the President's steadying it. The President repeated the process with the bowl for Marcus and then the bread platter. She then turned and looked into Mary's face and said, "They aren't a threat to you. They're friends."

"Yes, Ma'am," said Mary, who immediately fled back to the kitchen as soon as the President released her hand.

"That went well," said Annie. "Are you sure we're going to be welcomed here?"

"Welcomed probably isn't the right word for it," said the President, "but the good news is you have no fear of any harm coming to you. You're about as safe as a lion in a flock of sheep."

"This stew is very good," said Marcus appreciably after taking a bite.

"And I think I could make a meal out of the bread alone," added Annie.

"Yes, the food here is as good as you'll find anywhere. The ingredients are all procured locally and prepared as carefully as possible. You won't find better food in either world than you'll find here. Mind you, the service could be better."

The three exchanged small talk until the food was consumed.

"Would you like any dessert?" asked the President.

"I'm stuffed," said Annie.

"Me too," said Marcus.

"It's just as well. I suspect we've subjected Mary to enough stress for one day. Come, let's pay our bill and see about getting you two accommodations for the night."

The President led them back to the front desk which was empty. She rang the bell on the desk and waited for a few seconds before knocking loudly upon the desk.

"I'll come back there and drag you out if need be," threatened the President.

Annie thought of something and whispered it into the President's ear which produced a smile.

"Or better, yet," said the President loudly responding to Annie's suggestion. "I'll send my two friends in there to find you."

This latest threat produced the sound of scampering in the room, some hushed conversations, and finally the emergence of the proprietor who looked absolutely terrified. She stood in the doorway, clearly ready to flee back into the interior at the first hint of a threat.

"Ah, there you are," said the President breezily. "Now, what do we owe you for the dinner tonight?"

"Nothing," said the woman nervously. "There's no charge at all. It's fine."

"Now," said the President. "You know as well as I do that I have to pay. What is the charge? We had three bowls of stew and a loaf of your bread."

"It was delicious," said Annie.

Annie's words brought the briefest flash of a smile to the proprietor before the fear took back over.

"Three stews and a loaf of bread would be twenty Franklins," said the proprietor nervously.

"Franklins?" asked Annie.

"It's one of the names for our currency. We have Franklins, Edisons, Teslas, and more. Twenty Franklins would be the equivalent of around twenty dollars on your side."

"It was worth it and more," said Marcus.

The President counted out the currency and placed it on the counter. The proprietor stood back and never moved to take it, just leaving it there.

"Now, we'll need a pair of rooms for these two for the night," said the President.

The fear on the face of the proprietor now transformed into a look of sheer terror.

"Rooms? Here? For them?" asked the proprietor.

"This is an inn, is it not?" chided the President.

"We're booked solid," lied the proprietor.

"And yet I see at least two room keys hanging there," said the President nodding towards a key rack. "Or did you forget that?"

"Those rooms aren't, aren't, aren't necessarily suitable for guests of this stature," said the proprietor. "I'd assumed you'd want nicer accommodations for them."

"I seem to recall staying in room 312 the last time I needed a room, and it seemed perfectly adequate to me," said the President.

"You can't make me keep them here," said the proprietor. "They'll ruin my business! No one will want to stay in the same room they stayed in."

"Oh, for God's sake, will you get over this?" asked the President. "They're not dangerous. They are just a normal pair of humans here attending to the business of the council. You will provide accommodations to them or so help me, I'll shut this place down! Do we understand each other?"

"Yes, Madame President. If you order it then I'll comply, but I don't have to be happy about it."

"Now, if you'll show us to the rooms," said the President, "I can then leave these two here and pick them up in the morning on my way back to the council."

"Leave them here? Alone? All night?"

"That's what inns are for," reminded the President. "If you didn't wish to have guests staying overnight you should have gone into another line of work. The keys if you please?"

"One moment," said the proprietor before disappearing into the back room again. More muted conversation could be overheard and then Mary was once again shoved out to face the trio.

"Ah, Mary," said the President. "I should have known. It's nice to see you again. Would you mind showing us to the rooms?"

"No Ma'am," said Mary. "Just follow me,"

Mary picked up the two keys and then slid out from behind the desk keeping her eyes glued to Marcus and Annie as she slowly backed around them and over to the stairs. She never turned her back to them, and was clearly prepared to flee at the first sign of anything going wrong, as the trio followed a few steps behind her.

"We're really not dangerous," assured Annie once again.

Mary gave her a slight smile and then continued to back up the stairs.

"Mary's usually quite talkative and the life of the place," said the President. "I'm guessing we're catching her on an off day today. Is that it Mary? Have we caught you on an off day today?"

"This is all new to me Ma'am," said Mary quietly.

"It's all new to us too, if that's any help," said Annie. "We never even knew this place existed before this morning. Now we're here and people act like we're wild animals or something. We're really not dangerous to you."

"They're friends Mary," assured the President.

"If you say so, Ma'am. It's just that I've heard so many stories and things that it's hard to put aside the fear."

"And believe me, they've heard similar stories about our kind. What is it, the Hansel and Gretel story where a witch kidnaps and eats children?"

"Yeah, she lived in a house made of candy to lure children and then ate them," said Annie.

"Would you ever do that Mary?" asked the President. "Should they believe that's something you'd do?"

"Of course, not! Don't be absurd! I'd never hurt anyone and especially not children! It's unthinkable!"

"And they will not harm you," assured the President. "They're here to help us, not harm us."

"If you say so, Ma'am" said Mary as she appeared to relax a bit, though still ready to flee at any second.

"Here's the first room," said Mary holding out a key to the President who took it and then held Mary's hand for a second reassuringly.

"The other room adjoins this one?" asked the President.

"Yes, Ma'am," said Mary.

"Thank you Mary," said the President. "I'll get them settled in. Thank you for showing us up."

Mary turned and ran down the stairs.

"Come," said the President unlocking the first room. "Let's see what I've gotten you two into." She led the way into the room and lit a lamp nearby using a match.

"You needn't worry about running out of oil for the lamp," said the President after giving it a shake. "There's plenty there to keep it lit all night."

The President then checked out the bed and furnishings and nodded her head.

"I think this will do nicely. Let's look at the second room shall we?"

She opened the adjoining door and it was identical to the first.

"Excellent! I'm sorry again for keeping you here this long, but we weren't expecting your images of the book to be an issue. We should have an answer for that in the morning and then you can get back to your world. Is there anything else you need?"

Marcus and Annie could think of nothing. The President soon left them alone and Annie lay down in her room for about a half hour and tried to sleep, but it was impossible. She knocked lightly on the door connecting the two rooms and was surprised when Marcus immediately swung it open.

"Are you okay?" asked Marcus.

"Yeah, I'm just a little freaked out about everything that happened today. How are you?"

"I'm the same. It's been a weird day."

"Would you mind if we left this door open? I don't really think anyone here is a threat, but I trust you more than them."

"It's fine by me. I'm not sure I'll be getting much sleep anyway."

"Oh, god! How did all of this ever happen? I'm thinking I should have just thrown that book away."

"With any luck it'll all be over tomorrow."

Chapter Six

The Council President greeted Annie and Marcus early the next morning and led them back down to the dining room for breakfast. The dining room was empty. Mary shyly emerged from the kitchen and approached the table.

"Good morning, Mary," said the President.

"Good morning, Ma'am," said Mary, "Can I take your orders?"

"You look a bit calmer today," said Annie.

"I had a good long think about what was said yesterday and I realized I was judging you two by the stories I'd heard instead of by who you are. You haven't given me any reason to doubt you just yet, so I'm trying to give you the benefit of the doubt. It's not always that easy though. It's like suddenly being told a lion is just a big cuddly housecat and you don't have to worry about being in the same room with one, but I'm trying to adjust."

"You're doing wonderfully," said the President.

The three ordered their breakfast, ate it in relative peace and quiet, and then paid their bill at the front desk. When they arrived at the Council building, the Council's technical adviser was waiting for them.

"We've got a problem," he said.

"What is it?" asked the President.

"This smart phone has been compromised and now functions largely like the book. The e-mails sent to and from it have the same properties as the book and therefore this phone poses the same risk to us as the book does. Not only that, but the e-mails that were sent are likely to be just as dangerous. If they're widely distributed, we could be in much more trouble than we'd have been from the book alone. There are a finite number of pages in the book, but the e-mails could be produced in infinite quantities. We've got to get a handle on this."

"How do we do that?" asked the President.

"We need to get access to the e-mails that were sent and get access to the computers that sent and received them. It's relatively easy for us to immunize the devices once we can get access to them, but getting access to the computers and e-mails could be an issue."

"Could Wallace immunize the computers?"

"Certainly. He's very gifted with such devices."

"Do we absolutely know that these e-mails on the other devices are a problem?"

"We're pretty sure they are, but we won't know for sure until we can inspect the devices that received them and the e-mails themselves."

The President turned to Marcus and asked him, "How well do you know the people you sent the e-mails to?"

"I know most of them pretty well. We've met on multiple occasions. We ship books to one another if they've got a customer and I've got the book."

"Do you think they'd let you get close to their computers and other devices?"

"Probably," said Marcus. "The closest guy is in Boston. He runs a little bookshop there that specializes in early American writing. It's one of my favorite bookstores and I modeled my own store after his. I was a regular there when I went to college. I know him pretty well."

"We may need you to go there to see if we can resolve this. Would you be willing to assist us in this manner?"

"I don't want any harm to come to anyone here, but I do have my business to run. I've lost a day of business already. I can't afford to stay closed too long."

"Mr. Ripa could see to the operation of your store while you're gone," said the President. "He's very experienced at running businesses in both worlds and would assure that things run smoothly."

"I guess that would be okay," said Marcus. "You should be advised though that I know very little about computers. I can go there, but my ability to deal with a strange device would be limited at best."

"What about me?" asked Annie. "I'm good with computers and smart phones. Can I go too? I might be able to help."

"As far as I'm concerned you can go," said the President. "We'll be sending along a young man from our side named Wallace to assist in cleaning the devices you encounter and the two of you could work well together. Would you mind if Annie went along Marcus?"

"Not at all, but Boston's a pretty good trip."

"We'll take care of the travel. I'll have Mr. Ripa meet with you down the hall and discuss how to run your business while I firm up things on this side. Then we'll reconvene and send you on your way. Hopefully this will only prove that there's nothing to worry about, but if there is something to worry about then it's better to get a handle on it quickly."

Marcus spent several minutes talking with Mr. Ripa on how the business ran and it quickly became apparent that Mr. Ripa was well versed in running a business. Mr. Ripa then left them and headed for the portal to open the store. Annie and Marcus settled down for a few minutes until a young man, about Annie's age opened the door and joined them.

"Good morning, I'm Wallace," said the young man who was dressed in jeans and a t-shirt.

"Morning," said Annie. "I'm Annie and this is Marcus."

"So I gathered," said the young man. "There aren't typically a lot of your type wandering around our Council building. Are you ready to go?"

"I guess so," said Annie. "How long will we be gone?"

"It shouldn't take long. Boston's not that far away. It's a short trip up and back. It shouldn't take long once we're there. The sooner we get started, the sooner we get done. Let's go."

The three left the council building and made their way along different streets and after a few minutes they were at the port. A dozen sailing ships were moored to the docks while other vessels traversed the river.

"We're sailing to Boston?" asked Marcus.

"It's the fastest way," said Wallace. "Captain Smith of the Blueblood is expecting us. He's heading to Boston in a few minutes and we've got passage booked. He's used to your type so you don't have to worry about that. His crew may be more of a problem though. Your type are viewed as bad luck by many of our sailors and we should probably keep you below deck and out of sight during the trip to avoid a mutiny."

Wallace led them to the ship and the captain greeted them on the gangway and told Wallace to stash them in the Captain's cabin. Wallace left them there alone for a few minutes as he went back out to talk to the captain.

"We're sailing to Boston?" muttered Annie. "This is unbelievable. How long will this take?"

"It's going to take a while," said Marcus. "We've got to leave the port, sail downriver to the bay, cross the bay into the ocean and then work our way up the coast to Boston which is a good ways away. Two days, maybe three would be a reasonable estimate. Then we've got to come back."

"And I didn't bring any fresh clothes," muttered Annie. "That's just great. It's bad enough I'm wearing these clothes a second day, now I'll be stuck in them for a week."

Calls could be heard coming from the deck and the lines were cast off. The ship started to move away from the dock. Marcus looked out of one of the portholes and watched as the ship entered the river and pointed downriver. The city soon disappeared from view.

Wallace then came back in and announced, "We're almost there. We'll be docking in about ten minutes, and once the crew disembarks we'll get off."

"What do you mean we're almost there?" asked Marcus. "We just left Philadelphia and we haven't even reached the bay yet."

"You're thinking of how things work in your world. They work differently here. If you look out your porthole you can see Boston on the horizon. We'll be getting off the ship pretty soon."

Annie and Marcus raced to look out the porthole and sure enough, an old city was appearing. As they neared the dock they could read a sign that read, 'Hankok's Wharf, Boston Ma.'

"How the heck did we get here that quickly?" asked Marcus in astonishment.

"We were lucky the wind was with us," said Wallace. "Sometimes it takes twice as long. We had the wind and tide on our side this trip, so it went quickly."

"But a trip like this should take days," said Marcus.

"Only in your world, not ours," said Wallace. "Things connect differently here. We're not quite as linear as your world."

The sound of the crew tying the ship to the dock soon echoed through the cabin and then they could hear the crew disembarking. Wallace went on the deck to be sure the coast was clear, and then he led the pair off of the ship and into the port.

"Welcome to Boston. Where's your bookseller friend located?"

"He's on Hanover Street," said Marcus.

"Excellent," said Wallace. "Then we'll head to Mills Pond and use the portal there. It'll be the most convenient way to cross from this version of Boston to yours."

"How far away is Mill's Pond?" asked Annie.

"Do you see those two four story buildings just over there?" asked Wallace pointing to two of the tallest structures nearby. "Those are the mills. The portal we'll use is in the one on the left hand side. You'll want to stick close when we go in. The mills are incredibly noisy when they're running and they're nearly always running thanks to the levees."

As they neared the buildings Annie was amazed to see a large pond between the mill buildings. A stone dam separated the water in the pond from the nearby bay and a horse drawn cart was traversing the levee as she watched.

"What is this place?" asked Annie.

"The pond you see is called Mill Pond. It was created to give the mills a steady supply of water," said Wallace. "The tide fills the pond as it comes in turning the mill at the same time, then the flow out is restricted to extend the milling time during the slack tide. You'll notice the hills nearby, they don't exist in your Boston, neither does the pond or much of the water you see here. The hills were taken down to fill in the area behind the dam to create more solid land. Our population is small enough that we don't need the land, but the mills are important to us, so they survived here even after disappearing in your world."

Wallace led the pair into the mill building. The miller was busy tending to the mill and paid them no attention as Wallace led them down a set of wooden stairs and to a small dark room. He crowded them into the room and then paused for a second during which Annie saw another bright blue flash before he opened the door and led them back out. They were now exiting a janitorial closet in a men's room in modern Boston.

"And we're here," said Wallace.

"That is so weird," muttered Annie looking back into the janitorial closet. "How do you know there's not someone already in the closet when you come through?"

"We just know," said Wallace.

Annie looked around and saw the urinals lining the wall and groaned.

"A men's room?" asked Annie. "Seriously?

"Don't worry about it," said Wallace. "Few use this facility, that's why we have a portal here. Shall we get going then?"

"Yes, please," said Annie. "I don't want to have to explain what I was doing in a men's room if anyone caught me here."

"I think you'll find it's easier for a woman to explain coming out of a men's room than a man coming out of a woman's room," said Wallace with a slight smile.

Wallace led the pair out of the restroom and along a dark corridor to a set of emergency stairs that led to the lobby of the building they'd appeared in. They walked out onto the street.

Wallace pointed down the street and said, "That's where the Mill pond was on the other side. The hills you saw on the other side were over there, but as you can see they're gone and so is the pond."

Annie paused for a few moments to look around in amazement.

"And all of that water is gone?"

"Displaced more than gone," said Wallace. "The hills were removed and used to fill in the area to create more land. It's effective enough, but I like the hills better. I also like the old Boston better. Your side of the world is a bit busy for my tastes. Let's find this bookseller of yours and get on our way."

In seconds they were walking down the street towards the bookstore.

Wallace stopped them outside the door of the shop and asked, "How well do you know this bookseller?"

"Quite well," said Marcus. "I shopped here all the time in college and even in later years I used to make a trip or two up here every month or two to see what he had in stock. When I bought my own store he kindly gave me advice on how to run it. He's a good guy. We shouldn't have any big issues dealing with him."

The three went into the shop and Annie was surprised at how similar it was to the shop Marcus had in Philly. It could have been a near twin as the layout was so similar. Even the bell over the door was the same.

"Okay," said Annie. "So which one of you guys stole the shop design from the other?"

"I may have inadvertently copied a few things from here when I redid my store."

"Do you think? It's like a carbon copy."

"Carbon copy?" asked Wallace.

"You don't need to know," said Annie. "It's an old way of making copies from our world. No one uses it these days."

"Marcus my boy!" said a friendly voice from the back of the shop. "I had no idea you were coming! You should have called me."

"It was kind of a last minute thing," said Marcus. "I wasn't sure I was coming myself until earlier today."

"It must have been very early to have caught a flight up here by now. And who are your companions?"

"This is Annie, she's the owner of that book I sent you images of, and this is . . .um."

"This is my friend Wallace," said Annie filling the silence.

"Allow me to introduce myself. I'm Harris Booker, and yes the name Booker is real. Oh! Did you by chance bring that book with you? I'm dying to see it in person. The photos are absolutely mesmerizing. The quality of the workmanship is amazing."

"I'm afraid not," said Marcus. "The book is a bit big to travel with safely. It's the photos and e-mails I sent you that I came to talk to you about. Could I see them?"

"Certainly, my boy. They're on my computer in the office. Head in and make yourself comfortable. I've got a couple of customers in the back and I'll join you once they're gone. Oh, and more good news, I may have a buyer for the book if you can come up with a price. I was mentioning it to a collector client of mine and he seemed amazed by it. He encouraged me to discover the cost and let him know. I suspect you could pretty much name your price at this point."

"Does this buyer have a name?" asked Wallace.

"Yes, his name is Howard Letts. He's a good customer of mine and has a great deal of interest in early American books. I'll be right with you, just head into the office and make yourselves comfortable."

The three entered the office and Wallace closed the door behind them and hurried to the computer.

"Howard Letts?" muttered Annie.

"Most likely a relative of yours," said Wallace as he slid behind the keyboard. "You did say the book came from up here so it makes sense there would be a Letts or two around. Let's see what we've got here."

His fingers flew over the keyboard faster than Annie had ever seen anyone's fingers move and within a minute he slid back from the keyboard and rose.

"Okay, we're done here."

"Are you sure?" asked Marcus.

"The files were active to my presence and have been deleted. I've checked to be sure they hadn't been forwarded to anyone, or printed out and they haven't. I've immunized the computer so any trace of the files is now gone and we should be good to go."

Just then Harris entered the office and smiled to everyone.

"So, you want to see photos and e-mails you sent me?" asked Harris. "Let me just get the old girl fired up and we'll take a look at them."

Annie watched as Harris slowly entered his password and then used a fingerprint scanner to access the computer. She then saw a look of confusion cross his face as he looked for the files.

"What the blazes happened here?" asked Harris.

"They're gone from your computer too?" asked Marcus.

"They were here earlier. I was looking at them again just this morning."

"The same thing happened to me. Wallace here is a computer guru and he thinks it's some sort of computer virus or malware that does it."

"But I've got good software to prevent that from happening."

"Even the best security software misses some things," said Wallace with a smile.

Annie heard the word security and looked up at the ceiling of the office and saw the security camera there just as it was in the store in Philly. The camera would have recorded Wallace using the computer. She made eye contact with Wallace and then looked up towards the camera. His eyes followed her eyes and he frowned.

"Perhaps you'd let me take a look at it," said Wallace. "I'm pretty good with computers. I might be able to find the files. Perhaps it's just hidden them."

"It can't hurt," said Harris. He rose and stood behind Wallace as Wallace's fingers flew over the keyboard.

"Wow!" said Harris watching as screen after screen flashed by at a speed he'd never imagined. "How can you do that so quickly?"

"I get paid by the job not the hour," said Wallace. "So, the faster I work the more I get paid. If I was paid by the hour I'd work much more slowly." He slowed down, stopped and then rose. "No, I'm afraid the files are gone forever. And speaking of gone, we'd best be getting back."

"Yes, that's a good idea," said Marcus. "Thanks for letting us in. I'm sorry the files are gone from your computer too. I was hoping to see them here."

"It's not a big deal," said Harris still looking a bit befuddled. "Just call me when you've decided on a price. My buyer is very anxious to acquire that book. He says money is no object."

"I'll call you when we've made a decision," said Marcus.

The three made their way back to the street and started back the way they'd come.

"Thank you Annie for pointing out the security camera," said Wallace. "I hadn't noticed that. I erased the pertinent parts of the tape so our tampering with the computer is not visible."

"Did you learn anything?" asked Annie.

"The files were active which means they could be used against us," said Wallace. "I was really hoping they would be inactive, but they weren't. That complicates things a bit. We've got to track them all down now and remove them all. How many e-mails did you send?"

"There were a few," said Marcus. "I'm not altogether sure now what I sent where."

"We'll have to go back to your store and check your computer to find out. We'll need to immunize that computer anyway, so let's make that our next stop."

They returned to the basement of the building containing the portal and Annie waited outside while Marcus checked to be sure no one was in the men's room then the three walked into the closet within the men's room, closed and reopened the door and they were once again in the cellar of the grain mill.

"Come on, let's head back to the harbor. I believe we've made it just in time to catch our ride back to Olde Philadelphia."

The captain was waiting by the gangplank as the trio arrived and sent them below decks once again. Within minutes his crew could be heard arriving and soon the ship was once again on the move.

"This is an amazing way to travel," muttered Annie appreciatively.

"It's very efficient," agreed Wallace. "I must admit that I get frustrated with travel on your side of the world."

"Do you visit our side often?" asked Annie.

"I'm there nearly every day. My mother sends me to school on your side of the world so I can get a more rounded education than I'd get on just our side."

"That's how you know so much about computers then," said Marcus.

"I'm afraid that knowledge comes more from my side of the city than yours," said Wallace. "Your computers, cell phones, and devices are areas in which we've been able to share our capabilities with mortals like you."

"I don't understand," said Annie. "You're saying you guys are behind our technology?"

Wallace nodded.

"I don't believe it," muttered Annie.

"Talk to your engineers and scientists and ask them to explain exactly how your devices work. At some point they'll always say, 'and we don't really know what happens here, but we know if we do this then that happens.' Suffice to say, we are what happens there. A while back one of our kind figured out a way to capture some of our capabilities and bind it to objects. You call them integrated circuits and microchips, but they're simply containers holding some of our capabilities."

"Yeah, right," muttered Annie.

"Think about it," said Wallace. "A few decades ago your only way to reproduce music was through phonograph records, each record was limited in capacity and the quality of the sound. Now you can carry thousands of works in high quality in the palm of your hand. Do you really think that came about without help from our side? It's our abilities integrated into those devices that gives you those capabilities."

The discussion was interrupted by the ship turning and slowing as it neared the dock. Mooring lines could soon be heard being secured and the crew disembarked. The three headed back to the deck and Wallace paid the captain his fee and then the three headed back towards the center of Olde Philadelphia to the Council building for Wallace to give his report on what they'd found.

Chapter Seven

The Council convened upon hearing of the return and the three travelers now sat before them.

"And what did you discover Wallace?" asked the Council president.

"I'm afraid the situation is as we'd feared and perhaps even worse. The e-mailed photos were reactive to my presence and were viewable in my presence. I was able to quickly redact the photos from that computer and determine that they had not been forwarded or printed. That vulnerability is now repaired, but there are other e-mails out there that must still be tracked down. I'm also afraid the e-mails have apparently been viewed by a Mr. Letts. The bookstore owner apparently showed him the e-mail and Mr. Letts is now very anxious to acquire the book. I'm assuming he was capable of viewing the images on the e-mails and that's piqued his interest. We must act quickly to eliminate this vulnerability."

"And our guests?" asked the cranky old guy practically spitting out the word 'guests.'

"They were an invaluable asset on this mission," continued Wallace. "The fact that the bookseller knew and trusted Marcus made it easy for me to get access to the computer. I'd overlooked a surveillance camera in the office of the bookseller until Annie alerted me to it. I was then able to remove my tampering from the video files showing the office. Had she not informed me of that camera the bookseller could have seen me accessing the computer on his security feed and raised an alarm. They both played a crucial role in clearing up this issue."

"Had it not been for them initially none of this would have been necessary," muttered the old guy.

"Had it not been for them this book could already be in the hands of our enemies," reminded the Council President. "We owe them our gratitude. Now I'm afraid we might have to impose on them once more to help us recover the last of the e-mails. Can we count on your support in that mission?"

Annie quickly nodded her assent and looked to Marcus who hesitated before finally nodding his agreement also.

"Excellent!" said the Council President."I understand that you need to return to your Philadelphia to determine exactly where you sent the e-mails, is that correct?"

"I sent off multiple e-mails about the book, but I only sent the photos to a few of those, but I'm afraid I'm not sure who I sent the photos to. Wallace says he can determine that from my computer and he'll also need to immunize my computer."

"Then you shall return to your side of the world to gather that information."

"While they're doing that I'd like to sneak back home and get a change of clothes if possible," said Annie. "I've been wearing this outfit for two days now and I could use a change."

"That would be no problem. Wallace will accompany you through the portal and while Marcus and Wallace are seeing to the computer you can change your clothes and refresh yourself. Wallace will then bring you back and we can make arrangements for the next leg of the journey."

The three made their way back through the portal to Annie's Philadelphia and she found herself almost choking on the fumes when they emerged from the alley.

"Oh, crap!" she muttered. "My lungs got used to clean air."

"There is a difference," said Wallace. "But we'll be back in the clean air soon enough. Now let's head to the bookstore where Mr. Ripa should be awaiting us and then you can get some fresh clothes and we'll be on our way again."

Annie left the two at the bookstore and headed back to her home.

"Hey, Annie!" came a call from a familiar voice as she neared her front door.

Annie turned to see Marty in his familiar brown UPS uniform waving to her from across the street.

"I've got a package for you. Are you going to be home in a few minutes?"

"Just for a bit then I've got to go out again," said Annie.

"You'll be there for ten minutes?"

"Probably longer," said Annie.

"Great! I've got some deliveries to make here then I'll grab your package and bring it over. I should be there in five minutes or so."

Annie hurried up the steps and unlocked the front door. She turned around and locked it then stepped into the living room only to stop cold when she heard a strange voice address her.

"And you must be my niece. It's nice to finally meet you."

Annie turned to find two men standing nearby. Her hand reached into her purse fumbling for the pepper spray she always carried.

"Who are you and what are you doing here?" asked Annie as she backed away from the pair.

"There's no need to be alarmed. We're kin though we've never formally met. In fact, I didn't even know you existed until recently. My name is Howard Letts and this is my son Michael. Your grandmother never told us she had a granddaughter. You can imagine my surprise to learn from a book seller in Boston that I had a previously unknown niece who was in possession of a very rare and valuable book. I can see that you don't have it on you and a quick look around here hasn't revealed it, so would you mind telling me where the book is?"

"I don't have the book any longer," said Annie. "It's gone."

"And where exactly is it now?" asked Howard.

"It's gone. I sold it."

"Then why were you in the bookstore up in Boston earlier unless you're still trying to sell the book? Why didn't you tell the bookseller it was sold and no longer available? And why on Earth would you be there with Wallace? You see I know who Wallace is. I'm guessing he was there to help you sell the book, but why?"

Before Annie could answer her doorbell rang followed by Marty's calling out to her, "Hey Annie, I've got your package."

"I've got to get that," said Annie. "He knows I'm here."

"That's fine," said Howard as his son moved over closer to the door. "Get your package and then we can continue this discussion. But, I need to see that book. It's quite literally a matter of life and death and I won't take no for an answer."

Annie walked to the door and tried to compose herself, but she was shaken by this intrusion.

She opened the door and saw Marty looking back at her and holding out a package towards her.

"Let me sign for that," said Annie.

Marty was about to tell her that she didn't need to, but then he noticed the tone of her voice and saw that she appeared a bit distressed. He handed her the tablet and instead of signing she wrote him a message. He glanced down at it and then nodded.

"I forgot something," said Marty. "I've got another package for you in the back of the truck. Can you stay here for another five or ten minutes while I get it out and then come back?"

"Sure," said Annie nervously. "I'm not going anywhere."

"I'll be right back, sit tight."

Marty went back to his truck and pulled out his personal cell phone. He called a detective he knew who lived nearby to whom he'd just made a delivery. Within three minutes the detective was there and Marty showed him the tablet.

"I need help, call 911," had been written by Annie on the tablet.

"How well do you know this girl?" asked the detective.

"She's solid. This is real. She's a good kid. I would have called 911 but you never know how they'll respond, or if they respond at all. I'd just seen you so I knew you were nearby."

"Okay, so we've got a potential hostage situation. Are there any other hostages in there with her?"

"There shouldn't be. Her mom's off on vacation. She's alone. Look she's expecting me back any minute. If things work like they did the last time I can grab her and whisk her out of danger while you deal with the bad guy or guys. We've got a narrow window here to get this done. I say we move now and get her out of danger. Are you okay with that?"

"It might be our best bet. I've got back-up on the way. Let's try it your way and see what happens."

Marty grabbed a package from the back of his truck while the detective positioned himself near the front door. Marty crossed the street and rang the bell. He could hear Annie approaching the door and then she opened it.

"I've got your package," said Marty holding it in front of him. Annie stepped forward and when she was in reach Marty grabbed her, jerked her through the door and then hurriedly carried her down the steps and part way down the block shielding her with his body as the detective entered the home with his gun drawn. Marty stopped halfway down the block when he heard a loud bang and saw a bright flash of light. Police cars were now arriving on the scene and additional officers entered the house with their guns drawn.

"What the hell?" muttered Marty as he set Annie down on her feet and checked her. "Are you okay?"

"I'm just a little shaken. Thanks for coming back."

"What happened?" asked Marty.

"There were a couple of guys waiting inside the house for me. I'm sorry to get you involved in this, but I didn't know what else to do."

"You did good girl," said Marty as his detective friend emerged from the house shaking his head and rubbing his eyes. "You did exactly the right thing. I'm proud of you. That was really smart."

"Did you get them?" asked Annie as the detective approached them.

"No. They had a flash-bang, stun grenade or something like that. I don't know what the hell it was, but there was a bright flash and a loud bang and then they were gone. I got a pretty good look at them first though. They smashed through a window and took off. We've got officers out looking for them now. They won't get far. There's a bit of blood left behind, so at least one of them got cut going through the window. Do you know who they were?"

"They said they were distant relatives of mine, a Howard Letts and a Michael Letts, but I'd never met them before and they shouldn't have been in the house."

"Do you know where they're from?"

"I think they're from up around Boston someplace," said Annie.

"Do you know what were they doing here?"

"I'd just recently inherited an old book from my grandmother and I think they were here to steal it."

"Did they get it?"

"No," said Annie. "I've already sold it to someone else. They don't know that though."

Annie looked up and saw Marcus and Wallace running towards her and she hurried to them.

"Are you okay?" asked Marcus after embracing Annie. "We saw the police coming this way and heard a loud bang."

"They were here," muttered Annie. "The Letts were here. They came for the book. They were waiting for me in my house."

"Which ones were here?" asked Wallace.

"They introduced themselves as Howard and Michael Letts."

"Did the police catch them?"

"No, the Letts set off a grenade or something that made a bright flash and a bang and then they jumped through a window to escape. I'm glad to see you guys again."

The detective had now joined the group.

"I take it you know these people?" he asked.

"They're friends of mine," said Annie. "I had just gone home to change clothes before meeting up with them. We were supposed to meet up again in a few minutes."

"I own the used bookstore down the block," said Marcus.

"I recognize you. My wife shops there a lot. I'm assuming you bought the book in question?"

"I didn't buy it, but I helped in some manner in the sale of it."

"Could you describe how you helped in the sale?"

"One of his regular customers saw the book and bought it while Marcus and I were researching it," said Annie. "Can we get out of here now?"

"We'll be pretty busy here for a while. Our forensics people will need to go over the house for fingerprints and DNA evidence. We'll have to bring in someone to seal up the broken window. We'll likely be here for several hours."

"I've got to get going pretty soon and I wasn't planning on staying home tonight anyway," said Annie. "I was just here to pick up some fresh clothes. If you let me grab them now, can we get out of here?"

"I guess so. We'll still need to be able to get a statement from you later on."

"I'll give you my cell number. You can reach me through that. I just don't feel real safe staying here until you catch those guys."

Annie was escorted back into her house by the detective who took an initial statement from her and then stood guard outside her door while she changed clothes and packed a small travel bag with some essentials. She emerged and found the crime scene investigators collecting fingerprints and other evidence throughout the living room.

"Do you have everything you need?" asked the detective when Annie opened the door.

"I'm good. You've got my cell number if you need me. I hope you catch those guys quickly."

"We will. Just be careful out there. We've got a team coming in to board up the window and we'll lock ourselves out when we're done."

"I'll be careful. I should be safe with my friends though."

Marcus and Wallace were waiting for her outside and they regrouped and headed back for Elfreth's Alley.

"Are you sure you're okay?" asked Marcus.

"They just startled me. Knowing what I know of the Letts now, hearing that name freaked me out a bit. I also couldn't find my pepper spray. It had gotten lost in the bottom of my purse. Suffice to say it's not lost anymore. I've got it in easy reach and a couple of spares besides. They won't catch me off guard again."

"Good," said Wallace. "We're almost to the portal."

'Won't they know we're coming here?" asked Marcus.

"They probably don't know where the portal is these days, but they won't interfere while I'm around. You're safe enough for now. Once we get this situation resolved, the Council will deal with the Letts and you won't have anything to worry about."

Annie breathed a sigh of relief when she was back on the other side of the portal. Wallace led them back to the Council building where Annie recounted what happened once again.

"So, they know about the book, but they also know the situation isn't resolved due to Wallace being along," said the Council President. "We shall need to move quickly to resolve this before they put the pieces together. We cannot have this capability falling into the wrong hands. Given the history of the Letts, we can't let them gain the ability to expose us again to those hunting us. It's getting late. May I suggest you two stay here for another night and then in the morning we'll send you after the last copies of the message."

"I'd feel safer here than home," said Annie.

"I'll accompany you back to the inn in a few minutes then," said the Council President. "You'll be safe there. Wallace you may leave for now, but we'll need you in the morning."

The three made their way back to the inn and while the owner still retreated upon seeing them, there was a different reaction from the diners when they entered the dining room. All eyes turned to them as before, but instead of terror there was a look of confusion and amazement. Whispered snatches of conversation could be heard.

"She faced down two Letts single-handedly," muttered one couple as they passed.

"Any enemy of the Letts' is a friend of mine," could be heard being muttered from another table.

They took a table and the President smiled towards Annie and said, "I'm afraid our gossip network here is very well developed and word of your encounter with the Letts is a pretty hot topic."

"It's just nice not to have everyone terrified of me," said Annie.

Mary came out of the kitchen area and walked right up to their table.

"Can I take your orders?" asked Mary calmly.

"You seem a lot calmer today," said Annie.

"I'm working on it," said Mary shyly. "I still get the heebie-jeebies from time to time, but the saner parts of me are keeping them in check. May I recommend the pot roast today? It's excellent! I've been sneaking some from the chef every time I go to the kitchen."

"That sounds good to me," said Annie. The other two quickly agreed and Mary disappeared back into the kitchen.

"How scary was that today?" asked the Council President.

"It was scary," said Annie. "They didn't really threaten me, nor do anything overly ominous, but finding two strangers in your house is never a good thing. Hearing who they were and knowing what I knew from talking to you guys made it scarier. I'm just glad my delivery guy came around then and understood what was going on. He got me out of there to safety and I owe him."

Mary came out with her tray and walked right up to their table to deliver their food. She served the group and her hand only shook a little as she dealt with Annie and Marcus then she smiled, calmly turned and walked back to the kitchen.

"It's nice that you're being more accepted here," said the Council President. "But I did kind of enjoy having the place to ourselves when everyone was afraid of you."

"With any luck we'll be done tomorrow and things can settle back down," said Marcus.

"Wallace said that the other photos are in Atlanta and Charleston?"

"Yes, he said we should be able to hit both sites easily tomorrow. I must say travel here is much faster than I was anticipating."

"Our worlds connect in different ways and it's those connections that make it faster. I wouldn't worry about the Letts any longer. The Council has people looking out for them and if they show themselves they'll be apprehended and surrendered to your local authorities to deal with them. My understanding is that the local police force is very anxious to find them."

The three ate their meal and then Mary came back to their table.

"Would you like any dessert?" asked Mary. "We've got some delicious pies."

"I'm stuffed," said Annie. "It's nice to see you so relaxed around us though."

"I'm trying," said Annie. She looked around the restaurant to see if anyone was listening, but no one was. She then moved closer to Annie and whispered, "I love your clothes. Does everyone dress like that where you're from?"

"People pretty much dress however they'd like on our side," said Annie. "There's no real right or wrong. I dress for comfort while others dress following whatever fashion trend is hot and trendy. Have you ever been to our side?"

"No," said Mary. "I've always stayed here. I've been tempted to go, but it's a little scary."

"You'd love the stores on our side if you like my clothes," said Annie. "We have huge department stores filled with more clothes than you can imagine. There are smaller boutiques for pretty much any type of clothing you could imagine."

"All we have here is Madam Marie's for clothing," said Mary. "And I'm afraid her tastes and mine don't exactly align."

"Well, I'm rumored to be getting something like five million dollars in the near future, so we could go on a heck of a shopping spree if you ever find yourself over on our side."

"I'll think about it, but going through that portal is more than a little scary."

"If you decide to go, let me know," said the President. "I can send Wallace with you to escort you and serve as a guide. He probably won't hang around while you're shopping, but Annie would be there with you then. Wallace could then bring you back after you were done."

"I might take you up on that," said Mary who then left their table and disappeared into the back.

"I wonder how Wallace feels about you sending him here and there all of the time?"

"As son of the council President he expects to be called upon from time to time."

"He's your son?" asked Annie.

"Indeed he is and I'm very proud of him. He's a fine young man."

Chapter Eight

The trip to Charleston, South Carolina occurred nearly identically to the trip to Boston. They boarded the same ship in Philly and arrived in Charleston in less than a half hour. They soon found themselves wandering through the streets of Charleston in search of an old apothecary shop that hid a portal. The operator of the shop paid them no mind as they walked through the shop and out through the back into a small shed. The door closed and the room went dark followed by a bright blue flash and then Wallace opened the door and they were in Charleston on the mortal side and exiting a garage's side door.

"I swear I'll never get used to that," muttered Annie as Marcus led them off towards the next bookstore.

"It is a bit unsettling the first few times," said Wallace, "but after a while you get used to it. We could stay completely on your side of the world to do our business, but travel there is much more challenging. Airports, buses, mass transit, they're as foreign to us as this way of travel is to you."

"Yeah," said Annie. "I guess it is all just a question of what you're used to."

Marcus led them to the bookstore and the three entered to find the owner currently out of the shop on an errand but the girl behind the counter told them he'd be back shortly. They passed some of the time looking through the shelves and then something made Annie turn and look out the front window. She let out a gasp and hurried over to where Wallace and Marcus were looking through an old book.

"He's here!" muttered Annie.

"Who?" asked Wallace.

"Howard Letts! He was staring at me through the front window! When he saw me looking at him he took off, but he's here. He knows what we're doing."

"Stay here," said Wallace. "I'll go and take a look."

"Be careful," said Annie.

"Are you sure it was him?" asked Marcus.

"It was him. I'll never forget that face."

Wallace came back in and told them no one was there now but he moved them all deeper into the shop while they awaited the return of the owner. Annie positioned herself behind the two guys while peeking out to see if she could catch another glimpse of Howard Letts, but only the typical South Carolinians passed the shop's windows. After what seemed like an eternity, the shop door opened and the owner returned. Marcus led them out to meet him.

"Hi, John," said Marcus.

"Marcus! This is an unexpected surprise. What brings you to Charleston?"

"I sent you some e-mails a while back about a book that I'd come into possession of. I was wondering if we could take a look at those e-mails?"

"Certainly," said John. "It appeared to be quite a fascinating book. Have you learned anything more about it?"

"I've learned quite a bit, but I'd love to see those e-mails I sent you again if that's possible?"

"That's no trouble, come into the office and I'll pull them up for you. I can print you out copies if you'd like."

"That won't be necessary. My friend here is something of a computer genius and he can just send me back a copy of them if he can use your computer."

"I wish I was a computer genius," said John. "I'm on the phone to tech support a couple of times a week. I swear that buying a computer is the cheapest part of owning one. Let's take a look at those e-mails again. Did you discover how to make the ink visible yet?"

"I think so," said Marcus. "It was something quite unexpected though. I'm afraid I'm not at liberty to say how exactly."

"I'm guessing that's why you have a computer expert," said John. "He no doubt figured out some way to scan it or something. If I ever find another book like that written in invisible ink then you can expect a call from me, and I won't take no for an answer on how to make the print visible. There's my computer. Let me just log in and find the e-mails and we'll be good to go."

John sat down at the computer and after a few minutes he'd logged in, sorted his received e-mails by sender and had all of the e-mails sent by Marcus on screen.

"There they are," said John rising from the seat and letting Wallace in. John was about to say something to Marcus when he heard Wallace's fingers flying over the keyboard and he stopped and stared in open mouthed awe at the speed with which Wallace moved.

"Whoa!" muttered John.

"He's very good at what he does," said Marcus, taking John by the arm and leading him away from the desk. "I saw an old Twain in that case out front and I might have a buyer for it. Mind if I take a closer look while he's dealing with that?"

"If you've got a buyer for it, then I don't mind at all," said John. "It is pricey though."

"How pricey?"

"I've had it tagged at fifteen hundred, but I could go down to twelve for the right buyer. It's been appraised at seventeen five."

"My customer can afford that without a lot of trouble. Can we take a look at it while Wallace forwards the e-mails to me?"

"Actually, I'm already done," said Wallace. "It's all good."

"Great. Now about the book, how's the quality inside?"

"Not as good as I'd like, but better than I'd expected," said John. The two engaged in a brief discussion and examination of the book before Marcus agreed to inform his potential customer of the book and perhaps complete the sale. The three then left the shop and headed back to the portal.

"How did it go?" asked Marcus.

"It was no trouble at all. I removed the contamination and replaced the images with comparable images that were pure so he wouldn't even know anything had happened. To him the e-mails should still look the same, only now they're safe for us."

As they rounded the corner and started towards the garage Wallace slowed them and then stopped.

"Something's wrong," said Wallace looking around cautiously.

Annie and Marcus stopped and looked around but saw nothing. Then they heard a sound coming from the garage where the portal was located.

Howard Letts and his son emerged from the garage door and walked towards the trio. Annie drew back and reached into her purse for the pepper spray. Her fingers found it and she unlocked the cover while keeping it in her purse.

"So," asked Howard Letts, "what brings the son of the Council President all the way to Charleston with these two to visit a used book store?"

Wallace coolly replied, "I'm afraid you'll have to ask mother about that. I'm not at liberty to disclose that information."

"And what about you, my recently discovered niece, will you tell me why we're here, or are you already making plans to get us in trouble again? And fear not, I have no intention of getting within range of that pepper spray of yours."

"Just leave us alone," said Annie. "If you don't leave us alone I'll scream and the police will come running again."

"I'm not overly concerned about your law enforcement," said Howard Letts. "Though that quick exit we had to make did nearly cost my boy here a finger when he got a bit careless. It was clever on your part to use that tablet as a signal. That was very clever, indeed. You made me proud. It was something a Letts would do."

"Then you'll be thrilled to know I've been texting the police on my phone while you're talking, telling them to come here."

"It's a good lie, but unfortunately it is a lie," said Howard Letts. "Your phone is lower in your purse and your hand is wrapped in a death grip around that can of pepper spray. It matters not though as we're not here to harm anyone. We're simply here to offer our assistance. After all, we are kin. You see, we need to borrow that book of yours for a bit. I fear it contains information that we can't acquire elsewhere."

"It's like I told you before, I don't have it."

"Then why are you here if you're not trying to sell the book? I must see that book. You have no idea the danger we're all facing. That book may just contain the answer to a question of utmost importance."

"We have no need of your help and our business here is concluded," said Wallace.

"Is it then? Well then I guess we should let you get on your way. Oh, your portal here, it's oddly blocked in some manner. Perhaps you'll have better luck with the one over on Calhoun Street, though I doubt it. Well, then I guess I'd best be off. I'll be seeing you my niece. Understand though that I need to see that book. It's quite literally a matter of life and death and there's nothing I won't do to see it."

The three watched as Howard Letts and his son walked out of sight.

"What was that all about?" asked Marcus. "Can't we use the portal?"

"I'm afraid they've blocked it and likely the others in the area. Those on our side will reopen them in time, but we don't have a lot of time to waste. I'm afraid we'll have to finish our trip to Atlanta on this side of the world. It's slower, but it's our only real option at this moment."

"I'm not sure I have enough cash to fly to Atlanta and I'm lacking the necessary ID to board a plane," said Marcus. "I didn't think we'd need any of that."

"It's not a problem," said Wallace. "I can supply you with all that you need. But, we must hurry."

"How did they know where we were?" asked Annie.

"There are a few of our kind who are exceptionally perceptive and can find pretty much anyone, anywhere. They're called Seers and they prefer to associate with the darker sorts like the Letts. I suspect one or more of their colleagues is so endowed. Those two don't strike me as being overly perceptive. As long as they're following in our wake we can complete our mission. They'll know where we are, but not where we're going so we can stay a step ahead of them. Their coming along after we've cleaned things up isn't a problem. It's a nuisance, but not a problem."

A quick stop at a photo printing booth procured the necessary ID's for both Marcus and Annie to fly. Annie stared at her driver's license in awe.

"How did you get that out of the photo printer?" asked Annie.

"Suffice to say many of your advanced devices contain unique features we can access in time of need. All one needs to know is how to do so. I can print passports, drivers' licenses, and any other official certificate you need from nearly any device that contains a suitable printer."

"And this will work if someone checks into it?" asked Annie looking at her driver's license once more.

"It will. Your information is in the required computers and any check will show it to be absolutely genuine. The same is true for the cards I made for Marcus and I. They are unbreakable and absolutely true."

"Neat! I'm the first kid in my class to get a driver's license and I didn't even have to take the test. I'm beginning to like hanging around with you."

"On to the airport," said Wallace. "There's a shuttle flight between Charleston and Atlanta that's departing in two hours. I've booked us seats on the plane. We've got to get there soon though."

Chapter Nine

The trip to Atlanta was uneventful, though Annie watched as every person boarded the plane expecting to see one of the Letts get aboard. Wallace assured her that the odds of the Letts even knowing about Atlanta were slim. Their arrival in Atlanta and the trip into the city made all three of them appreciate the more magical travel options available on the other side.

Finally they arrived at the bookstore. The owner greeted Marcus warmly as they entered the shop.

"Marcus! Well if this isn't a pleasant surprise! What brings you to Atlanta?"

"I sent you some e-mails about a book a while back and I was wondering if my young friend here Wallace could take a look at them."

"I suppose so," said the bookstore owner looking a bit puzzled.

"It could be there's a Trojan horse hidden in the e-mails," explained Wallace. "If activated that exploit could damage your computers and cause you all kinds of trouble."

"Wallace is a computer security expert," said Marcus.

"By all means then take a look. The last thing I need are more computer problems. I swear I spend more on the computers here than I do on my truck. There's always something new causing chaos."

"I'll fix any issues I find and make sure things are running smoothly," said Wallace.

Annie kept her eyes peeled out the windows of the shop while Marcus did his magic expecting the Letts to appear once again, but it appeared they hadn't come along to Atlanta.

"That's it then," said Wallace as he stepped away from the computer. "Your files are all safe and you should have no problems."

"It seems to be working faster now," said the bookstore owner.

"I tweaked a few of the settings to optimize things for you. It should work well and you should be problem free for a while."

"I don't suppose I could keep him here?" the store owner asked Marcus. "A good computer guy is hard to find."

"I'm afraid he's a Philly native. I just didn't want your computer getting in trouble as a result of my e-mail."

"Well, I really appreciate it. You didn't have to fly all the way here though."

"It was no trouble," said Marcus. "I wanted to look at a Twain book in Charleston at the same time, so this was a short side trip."

The trio said their goodbyes and left the shop.

"Now," said Wallace. "We can fly back to Philly your way, or we can travel on my side. Which would you prefer?"

Annie and Marcus looked at each other and then both replied, "Your side."

"I thought so," said Wallace. "Come, our portal here is located a few blocks away. It's located near the old railway station. It'll lead us back to the train that will take us home."

"They had trains in the seventeen hundreds?"

"No, the train came along in the eighteen hundreds, but when Olde Philadelphia was expanded in the eighteen hundreds the train station was included. Whenever the city is expanded the expansion includes what's in that version of Philadelphia. We'll be arriving in the Broad street Station that was built in 1881. The last expansion of the city in 1884 included the train station."

The three made their way to the nearest portal and then emerged in the alternate Atlanta. Old steam locomotives greeted them upon leaving the portal.

"I'm afraid we're inland now so we'll have to rely on the train to get us back to Philly. It's a bit slower, but not bad. Stay here and let me make the arrangements."

He returned a few minutes later and said, "I've booked us a private cabin as we don't necessarily want the regulars to get too unnerved sharing a more public space with mortals. The conductor is letting us board early, so we've got to get a move on. Let's go."

Wallace led them towards the rear of the train where a conductor held open a door for him as he approached. The conductor stepped back warily as Annie and Marcus neared and then closed the door quickly behind them. Wallace led them to the private cabin and then locked the door and lowered the curtain on the door's window to prevent anyone seeing them.

"The train will begin boarding soon and then it's about an hour trip to Philly," said Wallace. "We'll let everyone else board and then get off before we get off. We should be back home in an hour and a half or less."

Annie peeked out the train's window as passengers suddenly appeared on the platforms and filed aboard. Then the train's whistles blew several times and great clouds of smoke enveloped the train as it started to slowly lurch forward. The smoke soon cleared and Annie was amazed at how quickly the countryside was flashing by.

"How fast are we going?" asked Annie.

"Fast enough," replied Wallace with a smile. "We could go faster, but the Council has decided this is the best speed. There can be safety issues with higher speeds."

"Safety issues?" asked Annie.

"You don't want to know," said Wallace. "Suffice to say things can get a bit scrambled. Everything's good at this speed though. We'll be getting there soon. Once again though, we should wait until everyone else has disembarked and then leave to avoid undue disruption."

Within an hour the train started to blow its whistle again and the train could be felt to be slowing. Smoke once again enveloped the train as it slowed to a stop and the whistle blew three final times. As the smoke cleared Annie could see the passengers disembark and leave the area.

"Okay," said Wallace. "Now back to the Council to report on our adventure and then we'll be done."

The three left the train and Annie marveled at the architecture of the old train station as they made their way back to the streets. After walking several blocks the Council building loomed before them once more. The guards stood aside to let the trio pass and Wallace then led them in to meet with the Council.

Wallace gave his report and the older wizard of the group nodded approvingly.

"So, it's done then?" he asked.

"The threat is gone," replied Wallace. "The electronic devices have been wiped clean and they no longer pose a threat to us. I should warn you however that we did encounter Howard Letts in Charleston and he blocked our portals there."

"You saw him?" asked the Council President.

"Annie saw him first out of the bookstore's windows and he then confronted us at the portal," said Wallace. "It appears we acted just in time. He told us that our portals there were blocked and they were."

"So it was him who did that?" asked the Council President. "We've already got a team working to reopen them. They should be restored anytime now. It was bold of him to confront you so openly. I had hoped the Letts and their lot were gone. It appears they were simply lying low instead. It's a pity they've now chosen to come out into the open."

"It's more of a pity for them once we catch up to them," said the old wizard on the Council.

"They're no longer lying low," said Annie. "He's been in Boston, Philly, and now Charleston in the last couple of days and he's confronted me twice."

"All because you had something he wanted," said the old wizard. "Since you no longer have it, he should leave you alone. I dare say even he doesn't want the Council to condemn him for any of his actions. Even though he lives apart from us, justice can, and will find him. There is no sanctuary in either your world or ours where he can hide from justice."

"What happens if he keeps bothering me?" asked Annie. "He seems very insistent on seeing the book. He says it's a matter of life or death."

"We will deal with him," said the Council President. "As you've seen gossip spreads quickly here and we've already let word slip that the book is in our custody and safely under our control. It is highly likely that the Letts will soon hear that the book is no longer under your control and they will resume their normal lives. If they fail to do so, then we will deal with them. If you'd like I could have Wallace create an app for your phone that would allow you to contact me directly?"

"That's not necessary," said Annie. "As long as they don't bother me, I shouldn't need to bother you."

"Now there is the matter of your payment for the services rendered," said the Council President. "Annie, we have arranged to make a sizable donation to a college trust fund for you that will account for a good portion of the money we owe you. Whatever funds you don't use for your college costs will be yours to do with as you please upon graduation. In addition to that we've created a line of credit for you that will give you the capability to spend up to another one million dollars in whatever manner you choose. All you need to do is present a debit card I've got for you to the seller and your sale will be covered. Wallace will install an app to give you an accurate accounting of the funds you have left.

"Now Marcus, I believe you and Mr. Worm picked out the books you wish to receive as compensation?"

"We did," said Marcus.

"They shall be arriving in your shop over the next few days with bills of sale and the required provenance. You will be able to do with them as you see fit."

"I'm afraid I may just keep them for myself. I'd find it very hard to part with them now that I've seen them."

"That is your choice to make," said the President. "Now the time is getting late. May I suggest we stop at the inn to get one final meal together before we send you back to your world?"

"That would be wonderful," said Annie. "I'm not sure I've eaten better food than that."

Annie, Marcus and Wallace waited nearby while the President finished her Council business and then the four left the building to go to the inn. Once again it was crowded in the dining room as they entered but a table was vacant in the middle of the room. Annie smiled at the difference in attitude this time as they entered. Smiles came to them from nearby tables. One older woman reached out and grabbed her arm and said, "Bless you my child for what you've done for us!"

Mary came out of the kitchen carrying a tray for another table and smiled upon seeing them. She quickly emptied the tray and then hurried over to them.

"Good evening Mary," said Annie.

"And good evening yourself," said Mary. "From what I've heard you've had a very busy day today, so may I recommend our porterhouse steak, some twice baked potatoes, and some chef choice options besides?"

"The porterhouse steaks here are to die for," said Wallace. "They don't hang around long when they get them, so I'd recommend taking advantage."

""Fine by me," said Annie.

"Excellent!" said Mary with a smile and then she turned and walked back into the kitchen.

She soon returned with a large tray covered with plates overflowing with delicious looking food. A huge porterhouse steak covered nearly half of the large plate and a potato roughly the size of a softball with a lake of melted butter in the center took up still more space. Side dishes piled high with assorted vegetables soon covered the table.

"Wow!" muttered Annie appreciatively. "That's a lot of food!"

"Well," said Mary, "the chef and I figured you'd built up quite an appetite with all of the traveling for us today, so we may have gone a bit overboard. Eat what you can and leave the rest. I would recommend trying at least one of the rolls though. They're divine."

The four dug into the plates with gusto and slowly worked their way through the food. Annie was among the last to stop eating and she only stopped when she couldn't cram one more bite in.

"It's a good thing I don't live here," said Annie. "I'd weigh a thousand pounds. That's amazingly good food."

"The clothes here do a good job of hiding some extra weight," said the president with a smile.

Mary came back out to pick up the now largely empty dishes and she asked, "And what would you like for dessert?"

"I can't swallow one more bite," said Annie. "That was just delicious."

"Are you sure," asked Mary. "We have some delicious fresh fruit pies."

"I just can't," muttered Annie. "I'm going to have to go shopping to buy some new clothes now as I think I may have outgrown these from this meal alone."

"I'd love to go shopping with you sometime," said Mary quietly.

"I'd love to have you come," said Annie. She reached into her pocket and pulled out the new debit card the Council President had given her. "Rumor has it I've got a million dollars on this baby to spend and you could help me spend some."

"Is that a lot?" asked Mary.

"That's an enormous amount," said Annie. "What about it? Would you like to help me spend some of this?"

"I don't know. It's kind of scary going to your world."

"I can take you back and forth," said Wallace. "I can even escort you to Annie's place and then wait there while you two shop and then bring you back."

"When would I go?" asked Mary.

"When are you off?" asked Annie.

"I'm off tomorrow, but I'd hate to impose that soon."

"It's not an imposition," said Annie. "It'll give me a chance to test out the new card and make sure it works. Can you meet up with me around ten tomorrow morning?"

"Can I?" Mary asked Wallace and the Council President.

"It sounds good to me," said Wallace.

"Just be careful over there and don't spend all of Annie's money," said the Council President.

Chapter Ten

Annie was dressed and waiting just before ten when her doorbell rang. She looked out and saw Mary and Wallace standing outside. Mary looked a bit nervous and kept looking around in awe at her surroundings.

"Hi guys," said Annie happily as she opened the door. "Come on in. I'm glad you showed up. I was afraid you'd change your mind."

"She almost did," said Wallace, "but I didn't give her a lot of choice. I think it'll be good for her to get a better feel for how both sides work."

"This is where you live?" asked Annie looking around and then marveling at the lights. "There are no flames!"

"Yeah, they're electric lights," said Wallace flicking on and off the wall switch as Mary stared in amazement.

"Wow!" muttered Mary.

"You haven't seen anything yet," said Wallace. He turned to Annie and said, "Show her the refrigerator. That's likely to totally blow her mind."

"You don't have refrigerators?" asked Annie as she led Mary to the kitchen.

""I don't know. What's a refrigerator?"

"It's like an icebox only without the ice," said Wallace.

"Seriously?" asked Mary. "You don't have to fill it with ice? That's one of my least favorite jobs at the inn."

"This makes ice," said Annie pressing a glass against the ice dispenser and filling it with ice and then cold water. "Would you like a drink?"

Mary had pulled back a bit at the sound of the ice hitting the glass and now eased forward and timidly took the glass from Annie and examined it.

"It's so pretty!" exclaimed Mary.

"I guess it is," said Annie. "We just take it for granted."

Wallace and Annie then led Mary on a tour of the house showing her the various systems and explaining how they worked. They ended up in Annie's bedroom where she opened her closet door to show Mary her clothes.

"Oh my God!" exclaimed Annie. "You have so many clothes! I've got five dresses and they're all pretty much the same. How do you find time to wear them all?"

"There are things here I've only worn once or twice. I mostly stick to maybe five or ten outfits that I'm most comfortable in. Would you like to try anything on? We're about the same size."

"Could I?"

"Knock yourself out."

Wallace excused himself and went out to watch TV while the two girls went through the closet.

"I like this top," said Mary easing a brightly flowered mini-dress from the closet.

"That's actually a dress," said Annie holding it up. "Would you like to try it on?"

"A dress?" said Mary eying it skeptically. "It's really short."

"In some quarters here this would be considered pretty conservative. There are girls who wear skirts that are far shorter than this. If it would make you more comfortable you could wear leggings, or a pair of tight jeans under it. Why don't you try it on and see how it fits."

For the next half hour the two girls went through many of the clothes in Annie's closet with Mary disappearing into the bathroom to change and then emerging to examine herself in Annie's mirror. In the end she liked the short flowered dress with tight jeans the best.

"Why don't you wear that while we're shopping," said Annie. "It'll make you stand out a bit less than your old dress."

"Is it okay for me to be seen out in public dressed like this?"

"You'll just blend in with everyone else," said Annie. "Let me add just a hint of makeup to you and we'll be good to go."

When they finally emerged from the bedroom Mary shyly stood before Wallace who gave her a quick look up and down and complimented her on how nice she looked. Mary blushed and then agreed that she was ready to go.

"Mind if I stay here?" asked Wallace. "I don't get much of a chance to watch TV and you guys probably don't want me around while you're shopping."

"Knock yourself out," said Annie. "There's food in the fridge and help yourself to anything. We'll be back sometime this afternoon, maybe sooner if the card doesn't work."

Annie led Mary out and down the street. Their first boutique was just a few blocks away.

"What did you mean when you said maybe sooner if the card doesn't work?"

"I haven't had the chance to test out this debit card the Council President gave me just yet," said Annie. "We'll buy something cheap that I can afford to pay cash for first just in case, but once I know it works then we can have some fun."

Annie had thought that starting out in a smaller boutique would be less intimidating to Mary than hitting a full-fledged department store and when she saw how Mary reacted she was glad she'd made that choice. Mary's eyes were wide as saucers as they entered the shop.

"Let's look over here," said Annie leading Mary towards the back of the shop.

Mary's fingers reached out and touched nearly everything in reach as she worked towards the back of the store as she explored this strange new world.

"I've never seen most of these fabrics before," muttered Mary. "What is this?"

"Some sort of a synthetic," said Annie. She looked at the label and then added, "It's a nylon acetate, whatever that is. I'm guessing it's some form of polyester. It's a very pretty dress though."

"We only have wool, leather, and cotton," muttered Annie.

"Polyester can be neat in that it's super easy to care for. You generally don't have to iron it, or do anything special care wise. Some people don't like it because it's synthetic, but it doesn't bother me."

"It's very pretty," said Mary.

Annie glanced at the tag and smiled. "It's your size. Would you like to try it on?"

"Here?" asked Annie looking startled.

"There are changing rooms over there. What do you say? If you like it we can test out the new card on it. It's in the right price range."

"I don't know."

A sales clerk came over and complimented Mary on her taste for liking that dress. Annie and the sales clerk were able to convince Mary to try it on. She shyly emerged from the dressing room a few minutes later wearing the new dress.

"Wow!" said Annie. "You look great!"

"It's like the dress was made for her," agreed the clerk.

"It's not too short," asked Mary. The hem came to slightly below her knees.

The clerk looked at Annie questioningly and Annie said, "She's a bit Amish in her normal dress, so that's pretty daring for her."

She then turned to Mary and said, "It's gorgeous and no, it's not too short. It's perfect on you. We should get it."

"It feels so good. Are you sure it's okay to get it?"

"Absolutely," said Annie.

Mary disappeared back into the changing room and emerged a few minutes later with the dress neatly hanging on the hanger once again and handed it to Annie. They followed the clerk to the register and Annie held her breath while the clerk swiped the card and then breathed a sigh of relief when the sale went through. The clerk bagged the purchase and handed the bag to Annie who immediately handed it to Mary and the two went out onto the street.

"That was amazing!" muttered Mary.

"Let me check something," said Annie as she pulled out her smart phone. She opened the app that Wallace had installed to monitor the account and saw that the cost of the dress had been deducted and showed her with a balance of over nine hundred and ninety nine thousand dollars still remaining.

"Did it work?" asked Mary.

"It worked perfectly," said Annie. "Come on, we're going to have some real fun now."

The two hit store after store over the next four hours and soon each was burdened with multiple bags as they emerged from a shoe store.

"How do they expect people to walk in those high heels?" asked Mary.

"It takes time and practice," said Annie. "I can get you a pair if you'd like."

"No thank. I think our shoes are a better option than those."

"What do you say we drop this load off at home and then head back out?"

"The bags are getting a bit heavy," conceded Mary.

Annie started to turn and head back to her home when she heard a familiar voice close by.

"Good afternoon ladies," said Howard Letts. "I take it you're spending some of your inheritance?"

"What do you want?" asked Annie positioning herself between Howard Letts and Mary.

"I just want to talk with you my niece."

At hearing the word niece, Mary turned white and gasped.

"I see your friend knows who I am. That's a shame for her."

"Don't you even think of harming her," threatened Annie.

"No harm will come to either of you as long as you come with me and do as I say. If not, then I'm afraid your little friend may have a very unpleasant time of things."

Annie looked back at Mary and saw Howard's son had come up behind her and put an arm around her waist. A closer look showed something sharp pressed into Mary's side.

"It would be a shame to have to kill her here. Neither of you will come to harm if you would just take a few minutes of time and join me for a brief conversation. You see, I meant it when I said I needed to see that book."

"I don't have it any longer," said Annie. "There's nothing to talk about. It's gone and there's nothing anyone can do about it."

"Be that as it may, I still need to talk with you," said Howard Letts. "You saw the book. You may have seen what I need to know."

"Let her go and I'll talk to you all you want," said Annie.

"No, I'm afraid that's not going to happen. She'll stay with us until this conversation is concluded. Now let's adjourn someplace quieter where we can continue our conversation. And if you should try to use that pepper spray you're so fond of, my son will be forced to make this Mary's last trip to this side of the world. Oh, and don't even think about using your smart phone to signal for help.

Keep your hands on your bags where I can see them. Now, will you come with us?"

"Do we have a choice?" asked Annie.

"Not really. Let's go then."

Annie's eyes darted around looking desperately for a policeman or someone to signal for help, but the streets were largely quiet with those few passing in too much of a hurry to get where they were going to pay her any mind. They walked for a couple of blocks before coming to a small bar in the middle of a block. It was almost unnoticeable being little more than twelve feet wide.

"In here," said Howard Letts holding the door open.

"We're under-aged," said Annie. "We can't go in."

"Go in, or she dies here," muttered Howard Letts with his patience clearly waning.

Annie reached back and took one of Mary's hands and then walked through the door into the bar.

"Okay," said Annie. "You wanted to talk, so talk."

"Not here," said Howard Letts motioning for her to go farther back in the bar.

"Not here? You kidnapped us and brought us here against our will and now you don't want to talk?" Annie said this loudly enough to make sure the bartender and the two other patrons at the bar could hear it.

All three heads turned towards them upon hearing her then they saw Howard Letts and nodded to him and went back to what they were doing.

"Clever girl, but this is my place and these people know me. Now walk out through the back."

"And then what?" asked Annie.

"And then we'll talk."

Howard gave Annie a shove towards the back and she reluctantly headed that way. She walked out into the alleyway behind the bar and turned around to face Howard Letts who ignored her until his son and Mary had also joined them. The door closed, Annie noticed a brief flash of blue light and then Howard Letts nodded to his son. His son reopened the door and led Mary back inside.

"I'm staying with her!" shouted Annie.

"Indeed you are," said Howard Letts. "Back inside you go."

Annie hurried to catch up to Mary and then realized something had changed. The bar was busier than it had been seconds ago and there was a different bartender. Not only that, but the air had changed somehow.

"What the? A portal?"

"Like I said, you're a clever girl," said Howard Letts. "Let's go then, back out the front and make a right. We're only a couple of blocks away from where we need you."

Annie led the way back to the street and instead of the Philadelphia from the seventeen hundreds she'd been expecting, this was one more from the nineteen twenties. Howard's son was no longer holding a knife to Mary's side now that they were someplace they felt safe, so Annie got close to her and assured her everything would be okay before talking to Howard Letts again.

"This is still Philly, but a different Philly again right?" asked Annie.

"Indeed," said Howard. "It took our side a while longer to figure out how to make a safe haven for ourselves but we finally did so and conveniently enough it arrived just as your prohibition era hit. Prohibition was a goldmine for us. Some of the busiest speak-easy's around were on our side of the portals."

"You open your side to mortals?" asked Mary.

"Indeed," said Howard Letts. "We'll let anyone through who has the money and meets our criteria. A lot of mortals need a safe place to retreat to, and we provide such accommodations at a fairly steep price and have done so for nearly a century."

"And you've kept it like this?" asked Annie.

"It's easier to keep a place like this as it was when it was created than remake it. That's why her kind still live in the seventeen hundreds era Philly. It's not so easy to change it once you've made it. Things can get a bit more unstable than you'd like if you try to change things. Come on now, where we're going is just up ahead."

The girls were led to a large building nearby and ushered into a dark office where a very old man sat behind a desk. The room was so dark it was hard to make out any of his features or even many details of the room. The two were shown chairs facing the desk and guided into them.

"Here they are," said Howard Letts before walking behind the desk and joining the old man there.

"Hmm. . . ." muttered the old man looking at the two girls, "you're definitely a Letts, but you, I'm not so sure about you. Perhaps an Albertson?"

Mary's gasp told Annie that the guess had been accurate and also confirmed it to the old man.

"Yes," he said. "I thought so. No doubt you're a serving girl then just like your mother. Well, we have use for girls like you here,"

"She's not staying," said Annie defiantly. "And how did you know who she was?"

"He's a seer," said Mary quietly looking even more afraid than she had been looking.

"A seer?" asked Annie.

"I'm afraid I'm not nearly as good a one as your grandmother was however," said the old man. "She had a special gift."

"You knew my grandmother?"

"She was my sister," said the old guy. "She was a few years older than I and much more capable. That's how she was able to take my book and keep it from me. The question is, why did she give it to you?"

"I don't know," said Annie. "I never met her. Now you'll let us go, or so help me God I'll get the two of us out of here no matter what."

The old man laughed before replying, "And how do you intend to prevent us from keeping you two? You're on your own here child. There's no one to help you. If we wish to keep Mary as a server here there's nothing you can do to stop us."

"I'll kill you all if need be, but you're not hurting her or keeping her. She's my friend and I don't abandon my friends."

"Well, if you do as we say there's no need for either of you to come to any harm," said the old man. "Tell me more about this book of yours."

"It's not mine any longer. I sold it."

"But you looked at it when you had the chance. What did you see?"

"I read a bit about Elf Reth and the Green Witch, but you already know about them."

"I need to know about the Green Witch's battle with the beast. I remember the book speaking of it, but I need more details."

"The beast? There was a drawing of her and a dragon?"

"That's the beast. What did it say about it?"

"It said something about she overpowered it. I don't remember too much of the story though."

"I need to see that book," said the old man. "I need to know how she overcame the beast. I need to see it myself."

"The book is gone and likely destroyed by now."

"It hasn't been destroyed," said the old man. "I'd know if it had been. You see, that was my book originally and your grandmother stole it from me when we were both young children. I'd confronted her about it a thousand times and she refused to relinquish it. For God only knows what reason she bequeathed it to you. Now I need you to get it back for me."

Annie now spoke very slowly. "I don't have it," she repeated emphasizing each word.

"I know you don't, but I suspect you could get it again. I need that book you see and I won't take no for an answer. I can't take no for an answer."

"Why do you need it?"

"That's of little concern to you. There's nothing you can do about what's to come, but if you don't bring me that book, then I'm afraid bad things will happen to your little friend here. If that doesn't motivate you enough then you will find that failing to comply will put others in your life in harm's way. Even your mother is not immune from harm on her cruise. We must have that book."

"Fine," said Annie. "Then we'll go back and see if we can get it for you."

"No," said the old man. "You'll go back alone and your friend will remain here as collateral. When you return with the book, we'll return her to you."

"And what if I can't get the book?"

"She's a serving girl, she can serve us as easily as the others. The clientele here is a bit less, shall we say polished, than what she's used to, but she'll adjust. Others have before, others will later. But, you'd best not fail or the repercussions for you and your mother will be quite severe."

"And if I go to the police?"

"And tell them what? That a wizard has kidnapped your friend? They're no threat to us. We're immune from them here. That's why this world is so popular with certain types. Howard here will return you to the portal. Once you've gotten the book, return to the portal and give this token to the bartender." He handed her a small gold coin. "He will then activate the portal for you. Bring us the book and you'll both go free and be bothered by us no more."

"What if I tell the Council of this?"

"I dare say the more perceptive of them already know. It matters not. They cannot touch us here. We don't fear the Council."

"Mary?" asked Annie looking at Mary.

"Go, but don't dawdle," said Mary. "I'll be okay. Just don't forget me."

"I'll be back as soon as I can," said Annie.

Howard Letts led Annie back to the portal and Annie soon found herself back in her Philadelphia. She ran to her home and burst through the front door startling Wallace who was busily watching television.

"You scared me!" muttered Wallace.

"They took her!" gasped Annie as she tried to catch her breath.

"Mary?" asked Wallace.

Annie nodded her head.

"Who took her?"

"The Letts," muttered Annie.

"Where are they?" asked Wallace.

"They made their own version of Philadelphia and they're holding her there. They want me to bring them the book to get Mary back."

"No," said Wallace. "That can't be right. They don't know how to create their own world. They're not that powerful."

"I've been there," said Annie. "It's like Philly in the nineteen twenties. I know where their portal is and they gave me this token to use to get back when I've got the book."

Wallace examined the token and then frowned.

"We've got to tell the Council," said Wallace. "This won't be pretty. Let's go."

They quickly made their way back to Wallace's Philadelphia and ran through the streets to the Council building. Wallace and Annie were stopped by the guards and held until the Council President was summoned.

"What's going on?" asked the Council president.

Annie quickly explained and Wallace chimed in with what he knew. The Council president examined the golden token and also frowned.

"Come, we must inform the full Council of this development. If proven true then it portends a great threat to our community."

Annie repeated what she knew before the whole Council and it created quite the buzz among the members.

"Well," said the cranky older guy. "We knew this was coming eventually. It was just a question of time until they equaled our capabilities. Now we must decide how to move forward."

"I need that book back," said Annie.

"That's impossible," said the Council President. "It poses too large a threat to the community at large."

"I'm not leaving Mary there with them," said Annie. "I'll tear this world apart if need be to find that book, but I'm taking it back and getting Mary back."

"There may be an alternative," said the older Councilman. "I believe I can alter the book in such a way that it'll appear to be functioning as expected, but in fact be under my control. As long as I live the book will appear to be acting exactly as they expect. But, with my death the book will revert to being harmless."

"But that will leave them with a weapon against us until you die," said the Council President.

"My death is not far off," said the old man. "There is little enough tying me to life here now. Allow me this one final service to the Council and the community. Once Mary has been returned and is safe here, I'll move on to that which lies beyond and the threat will expire before it can be used against us."

"I cannot order such a move," said the Council President.

"I'm not asking you to order it, but to allow this old man to offer one final service. Allow me to serve the Council and the people here one final time. It is no great loss. My end is near no matter what."

"You can alter the book so it will pass inspection?"

The old man grinned widely before replying. "There is no chance they will detect the alterations I'll place upon the book. It will appear as they wish it to appear and will do so until I pass. Assuming this young woman is capable of maintaining the façade while she hands the book over, then this will work. I fear though that we must stage things here to make it look as though the book was stolen from us. A few well placed rumors of Annie stealing the book back from us should suffice. I dare say they've got spies in this world and if they do so, then having rumors spreading here of the theft of the book will only lend credence to the book's provenance. She shall need an accomplice though. May I suggest young Wallace?"

"It would be an honor," said Wallace. "I wish to see this world they've created. Being implicated in the theft of the book should give me some access that I might not have otherwise."

"Do you understand the risks involved Annie?" asked the Council President.

"It's not like my life is especially risk-free now," said Annie. "They're threatening me, my friends and my mother. I say we end this thing however we can. I told Mary I'd get her back and I will."

The Council President sat and stared into space for several minutes before nodding her approval.

"We shall do this then. It'll take us a few minutes to alter the book and make the necessary arrangements then we'll see if we can pull this off."

Annie and Wallace were led out to the waiting area and after a half hour the Council President arrived bearing the book and the gold token Annie was given.

"Are you sure you both wish to do this?" asked the council President.

"I made a promise and I don't break my promises," said Annie. "You can take back the money you gave me, you can take back everything, but I'm not leaving Mary there with them."

"Here is the book and here is your token also," said the Council President. "Hopefully this all goes smoothly. Now to make this work, we're going to have to make your departure a bit more dramatic than typical. The guards don't know that this is staged. You'll be given a head start and then we'll notify the guards that you've stolen the book and must be stopped. You must run as you've never run before to get to the portal before they can catch you. We've got to make this look good to get the gossip going."

"How fast can you run?" asked Wallace.

"With people chasing me, I can run faster than anyone you've seen."

Chapter Eleven

"Stop them! They're thieves!" shouted the Council President as she raced out to the front door of the Council building and pointed towards Annie and Wallace who were sprinting across the square after leaving the building with the book in their hands. The guards immediately took up the chase yelling for the pair to stop.

Annie and Wallace were nearly across the square when the cries rang out. Annie looked back and saw the two guards running after them in a full sprint, but they had enough of a head start to stay in front of the guards. Wallace was carrying the book and leading the way to Elfreth's Alley. The calls of the guards were drawing attention from the residents. Curtains were being pulled back and people were looking out as Wallace and Annie ran past.

They were nearly to safety when Wallace stumbled on a cobblestone and Annie almost ran into him dodging him at the last possible second. She slowed for a second while he got back on his feet and up to speed, but that little hesitation let the guards really close the gap between them. They hurried into Eflreth's alley and to the portal and then paused while Wallace stared up at the busybody mirrors.

Annie watched as the guards tore closer and then looked to Wallace and up to the mirrors. She saw a brief flash of blue light and dove into the nearby alleyway between houses where the portal was housed. Wallace followed along behind her and stared at her in amazement.

"How did you know to enter the portal then?" asked Wallace.

"I saw the flash," said Annie. "The guards? They can't come through?"

"No, they're restricted to their side of the portal. They can't pursue us here. You saw the flash?"

"Well, duh! I've seen it every time. I'm becoming something of a regular with portal jumping so I now know when the portal opens."

"That's quite amazing. Come. We've got to get the book to the Letts and get Mary back."

"You're sure the guards won't come through the portal after us?" asked Annie.

"The guards won't come through," said Wallace, "but others might. We'd better get out of the area soon anyway just in case someone does. We should be able to elude anyone who hops over with little trouble anyway. This is your world after all."

"What happened back there when you nearly fell?"

"I slipped on a cobblestone and tweaked my ankle. I should have been better than that."

"I'm just glad it wasn't me. In the movies it's always the girl who sprains an ankle. Is your ankle okay?"

"It'll live," said Wallace. "Let's get this book to the Letts and get Mary back."

Annie led Wallace to the bar and the two went inside. The same bartender stared at the two as Annie walked up to the bar and handed him the token.

"Mr. Letts said only one would be coming back," said the bartender.

"I needed help getting the book," said Annie. "Wallace made it possible for me to get the book. Without him I would have never gotten it. The others are now hunting for him. I can't leave him behind or they'll get him. He's coming with me."

"Let me make a call," said the bartender pulling out a cell phone.

She eavesdropped on the bartender's side of the conversation.

"She's back but she brought a kid with her. She says he helped her get the book and that the others are hunting him now. She wants to bring him across with her."

He paused for a few seconds while the other party talked and then responded.

"All I know is what she said. I did hear a rumor that there was some trouble on that side and that they're looking for someone here. Do you want me to let him through?"

He then held the phone for a few more seconds before saying, "Okay."

"So?" asked Annie.

"Both of you can go through. Go out back, wait a few seconds and then come back through."

Annie and Wallace then walked out through the back and closed the door. They waited for a few seconds with Wallace watching Annie intently. Annie saw the flash and nodded to Wallace who reopened the door and they found themselves in the alternate bar. Annie quickly led them out and onto the street.

Wallace was looking around like a sightseer taking in all of the sights.

"So what do you think?" asked Annie.

"It's impressive," said Wallace. "I'm not sure how filled out it is, but what they've done is impressive. Where are we going?"

"It's just up ahead."

An older woman with a younger girl following behind her swept past them. The girl and Wallace made eye contact and then the girl quickly looked away.

"Sarah?" called out Wallace. The girl ignored his call and hurried up behind the older woman and tried to hide alongside of her. The woman stopped and glowered back at Wallace before turning to the girl.

"Do you know that young man?" asked the woman of the girl.

"No, Ma'am," said the girl nervously. "I thought I did from the past, but no."

She stared at Wallace for a few moments and then hustled off with the girl in tow once more.

"Who was that?" asked Annie.

"A girl from our world who we thought had drowned in the river," said Wallace. "She disappeared last summer. We knew she wasn't still in either world and had assumed she'd drowned, but we didn't know this world existed. I'm guessing she's been here since then."

"She didn't look happy."

"No, and that woman wasn't her mother. I don't know what's going on there, but something's up. I wouldn't trust anyone here if I were you."

"I don't trust anyone, anywhere right now," said Annie. "Come on, let's try to get Mary back first and then go from there."

Annie led Wallace to the building where she'd left Mary. Howard Letts was waiting outside for her.

"I see you got the book," said Howard Letts.

"It wasn't easy," said Annie. "I never would have gotten it without Wallace's help. Where's Mary?"

"She's inside waiting for you. We'll make the exchange there. Come on in."

He led the two inside and Mary was still sitting in the same office as she'd been when Annie left. Annie was pleased to see the relief in Mary's eyes when she saw the two of them.

"Are you okay?" asked Annie to Mary.

"I'm just a little scared," said Mary.

"It's okay. I got the book. We'll get you out of here."

"I need to see that book first though," said the older Letts behind the desk. Wallace handed it over to him.

The old guy examined the exterior of the book, opened the book and leafed through page by page and then examined the exterior one more time before looking back up.

"It all seems to be in order. Tell me, how did you acquire it?"

"Wallace showed me where they were holding it and he distracted the guards while I took it. We'd nearly made it out of there when someone noticed it was missing and notified the guards. We then had to run for our lives to make it to the portal ahead of the guards."

The old guy stared at her after she'd finished talking and Annie met his gaze unflinchingly. He finally looked down at the book once more and nodded.

"A deal's a deal," said the old guy nodding towards Mary. "You're free to go."

Mary and Annie rose and headed towards the door, but Wallace stayed seated.

"And what if I don't want to go back?" asked Wallace. "I think I could like it here."

Annie and Mary froze at the door and stared at Wallace in disbelief.

"Why would you want to stay here?"

"I think I have some things I can offer you. I could prove to be a valuable ally."

"And what can you offer us?" asked the old guy eying Wallace.

"A longer lasting version of that book," said Wallace. "You see Councilman Harris changed your book so it'll die when he does. I've got a copy of the digital version that will last forever as it was made before he changed it."

"I knew this came too easily," said the old guy patting the book. "Not that it matters. We'll get what we need from the book within minutes. That old fool Harris will die for nothing. Why did he do this?"

"The Council hoped you'd fall for this gambit," said Wallace. "Then Councilman Harris would pass and the book would become useless. What I've got is immortal. It won't die when the Councilman does."

"Why are you offering this to us?" asked the old guy.

"I like what I've seen of this world and I don't fit in either of the other ones. I need a way to buy in here and this data is my buy-in."

The old guy nodded to Howard Letts and said, "Give the young women back their bags and show them back to their world while Wallace and I discuss this and other matters."

Annie and Mary were handed their shopping bags and escorted back to the bar where they'd entered the world and were soon back on the streets of modern Philly.

"What just happened there?" asked Annie

"I don't know," said Mary. "Why would he do that?"

"He said he recognized a girl as we went in. He said everyone thought she'd drowned in your world."

"Sarah?" asked Mary.

"I think that is what he called her. Why?"

"She's his sister," said Mary. "We've got to get back and talk to the Council President."

"That would make Sarah the Council President's daughter? Wow!"

"We have to tell the Council President she's still alive."

"I'm thinking it's probably a bad idea for me to go back there what with everyone wanting me dead for stealing the book, but she'll need to know her daughter is alive."

"The President will make it all right once you see her."

"That's assuming we can get past the guards and residents who want me dead to see her," said Annie. "I'm thinking it's smarter for you to go back on your own and clear things up."

"There's another problem too," said Mary. "I can't open the portal."

"Hang on a minute. You can't open the portal?"

"No, I've never learned how to do it. Wallace is needed to open the portal."

"And he's not here. Oh crap! This just gets better and better."

Annie stopped and stood still for a few seconds looking around and then an idea came to her.

"Wait a minute. I might know a way to get you back there safely. Come on. Follow me."

Annie led them to Marcus's used book store. "Let's head in here for a minute."

Chapter Twelve

Marcus heard the bell over his door tinkle and he turned to see Annie and Mary walking in.

"Well, this is a pleasant surprise! What brings you two here?"

"I need your help again," said Annie. "We're in trouble."

"Please tell me you don't have another magic book?"

"No," said Annie. "But, we really need to make contact with Mr. Ripa. And believe me I mean we really need to make contact with him."

"What happened?"

For the next few minutes the two filled him in on everything that had gone down and he took it all in before shaking his head and replying.

"So you're both trapped here now and Wallace is one of the bad guys and staying in yet another version of Philadelphia?"

"That's where things stand now," said Annie. "We've got to get Mary back home so she can talk to the Council President and square everything away, but she can't get through the portal without help and Wallace isn't available. We know Mr. Ripa comes and goes and he shops here. We need to make contact with him so he can take Mary back and she can tell everyone what happened."

"I've got a phone number now to reach him," said Marcus leading them into his office to the computer. He dialed the number and waited for Mr. Ripa to answer. It went to voicemail.

"This is Marcus down at the bookstore. I've got Annie and Mary here and they need your help. We need you to get down here as soon as you can. Thanks."

"I hate voicemail," muttered Annie.

"What happens now?" asked Mary.

"Good question," said Annie. "I'm thinking we should head back to my place and get some food and something to drink before we start the next leg of this journey." She turned to Marcus and asked, "You've still got my number?"

"I'll call you as soon as I hear anything," said Marcus.

Annie led Mary back to her house and the two were resting after getting some food and water when there was a knocking at the door. Annie looked out the peephole and saw Mr. Ripa and Marcus there. She opened the door and let them in.

"Mary!" said Mr. Ripa. "It's so good to see you again girl! I was afraid you were gone forever."

"I would have been if not for Annie and Wallace."

"Where is Wallace?"

The two girls now told Mr. Ripa everything that had happened and he stared at the two in amazement until they'd finished.

"Sarah's alive?" muttered Mr. Ripa. "That's incredible! You said she was trying to hide though?"

"It was like she was afraid she would be recognized," said Annie. "Wallace was sure it was her though."

"We've got to get back and report this to the Council," said Mr. Ripa. "They need to know what's going on."

"No offense," said Annie, "but I may sit this trip out. The last I saw the guards they weren't overly friendly towards me and I'd just as soon not get killed. It's been a really long, long day too."

"Don't worry about the guards," said Mr. Ripa with an amused smile. "We can get you past them without much trouble. Mary, did you come here in your typical clothes?"

"Yes, why?"

"I'm thinking we can use them to disguise Annie to limit her exposure."

"Say what?" asked Annie.

Over Annie's loud objections and protests she was soon stripped of makeup and jewelry and had Mary's large and heavy dress pulled on over her jeans and t-shirt. A hat hid her hair and a scarf hid all but her eyes. Mary and Mr. Ripa observed her from all sides and nodded in agreement that she was unrecognizable.

"She might as well be in a burka," said Marcus. "She's unrecognizable."

"You dress like this all of the time?" Annie asked Mary.

"Not the scarf, but otherwise, yeah."

"No wonder you like our clothes so much. What about Marcus? Don't we have to camouflage him too?"

"It's not necessary," said Mr. Ripa. "Quite a few of our men come and go and they dress similarly. He's not as noticeable. Besides, he didn't steal the book. I can explain his presence pretty easily. Are we ready?"

"You're going to have to move more slowly with me wearing all of this," said Annie. "If you keep up the same pace as before I'll be left in the dust. These clothes feel like they weigh a ton."

The four made their way to the Elfreth's Alley portal and soon found themselves on the other side. Mary dressed in the modern clothes got a few people's attention, but then they recognized her and relaxed. Few noticed Annie hiding under her many layers of clothing. She might as well have been invisible. The Council building now loomed before them. Mr. Ripa excused himself and hurried in past the guards to inform the Council of their arrival.

Annie hid behind Mary and Marcus as the guards eyed the trio suspiciously. She was ready to bolt should the guards come towards them, but how effective she could be in getting away wearing a ton of clothes was up in the air.

The Council President soon came out and guided them inside.

"What happened?" asked the President. "Where's Wallace?"

Annie and Mary spent a few minutes relating the events and then finished and watched the President for a reaction.

"Sarah's alive?" she asked in disbelief.

"That's what Wallace called her," said Annie, "but I don't know if that's who she really was or not."

"Wallace would know," said the President. "I'll bet he stayed there to try and find her."

"But he gave them the digital copies of the book."

"Which means nothing," said the Council president. "We can deal with that. He needed a reason to stay behind once he'd seen her so he invented that. It was very clever of him. We've got to go and get them both. If they took my daughter against her will then it is a declaration of war. We've got to find out what's going on and put an end to this."

Annie started to say something then stopped and the council president noticed this.

"What is it? Is there something else?"

"It's just," said Annie before stopping. "It's just that I'm not so sure they took your daughter."

"What do you mean?"

"She had a weird expression on her face when she saw Marcus and I knew I'd seen it before but I couldn't really put a finger on it, then I remembered. It was the same expression I saw in the mirror a few years back when I got in trouble. You're happy to see someone then instantly mortified that they have to see you in this state."

"Can you elaborate on that a bit?"

"A few years back I had a bit of a crush on a guy a few years older than me. Mom was opposed to it and warned me away from him, so I told her it was nothing and

I wasn't seeing him, but every chance I got I would sneak off to be with him. Suffice to say we got arrested trying to sneak into a club and he called his parents to come and bail us out only when they showed up he threw me under the bus, blamed everything on me and I was left there alone. I had to call Mom to come and get me and while I was happy to see her, I was mortified that she had to come to get me from the police station.

"I saw myself in the mirror as I was leaving the precinct house and the look on my face was the same one your daughter was wearing. She was both happy to see Marcus, but mortified that he had to see her like that. I don't know what your daughter's personal life was like here, but I'm thinking maybe, just maybe she got involved with the wrong people and ended up there by choice, or circumstances."

"Sarah was a very good girl who would avoid trouble. Mary knew her. Isn't that right Mary?"

Mary's hesitation caught the President by surprise.

"Is there something I should know?" asked the President.

"I don't know if it's related to this or not, but Sarah was seeing a guy she met in school," said Mary. "They'd gotten quite close. She'd tell me about him, but claimed he couldn't come here. I'd assumed he was mortal, but he could have been one of those from the other side. She talked of leaving here and going to live with him, but I thought it was just talk. Then when she went missing and the word spread that she'd drowned I just assumed she'd drowned. If she's alive and over there, then she might have gone because of him."

The President collapsed in a chair and looked at the two girls in shock.

"She kept this from me?"

"Most girls keep lots of secrets from their parents," said Annie. "At least in my world, I'm guessing it's the same here."

Mary nodded her head in agreement.

"But, to let me think she'd drowned? Why put me through that?"

"Maybe she didn't think there was a better alternative," said Annie. "To be honest, I would have almost preferred being thought dead over having to explain what happened to my mother when I got in trouble. Kids don't always think things through and if she wanted to be with that guy, then chances are that desire consumed her thoughts. I just don't want you going to war if war's not what's called for here."

"But what is the right course?" asked the President. "My children are living among our sworn enemies. I don't know if they're being treated well or harmed. I don't know if they're being held hostage or not. I need to know what's going on."

"Maybe that's why Marcus chose to stay behind, to find out what's going on?" said Annie. "Maybe he'll report back and let you know."

"Maybe," said the President. "But I can't rely on maybe. It's getting late now, but Annie, I want you to take me to the portal to their world tomorrow and I'll see if I can't find a way to get through it. I'll reach out to their leadership on the other side and we'll see if we can find some common ground. A war would be bad for both sides and even your world which would be caught in the middle. Return to your home now, I'll have Mr. Ripa escort you and I'll meet you there tomorrow morning and we'll see if I can find a way to the other side to find out what's going on."

Chapter Thirteen

Annie was already up, dressed and waiting when the knock came on her door at nine the next morning. She let in the council President. Annie was relieved to see she wasn't dressed in combat uniform but more typical modern clothes.

"Mary and I talked yesterday after you returned home and she informed me that she was treated fairly well on the other side and thinks that my children are being properly cared for."

"I hope so," said Annie.

"But I need to see for myself what's going on. Would you mind taking me to their portal?"

"Let's go," said Annie.

The two wound their way through the city streets until they were outside the bar which was now closed and the doors locked.

"This is it," said Annie, "but it's closed until eleven."

"For some perhaps, but not for us," said the Council President. She wriggled her fingers before the lock and the door sprang open.

"That's handy," said Annie admiringly. "I wouldn't mind learning how to do that."

"Wait a minute before entering. There's an alarm and surveillance cameras that need to be deactivated." A few more hand gestures and some quiet words spoken so they were just inaudible to Annie and the red lights on the alarm pad and on the surveillance cameras went out.

"Okay," said the council President. "It's now safe to enter."

Annie led the President to the back door and the President once again opened it with no trouble.

"And this is it," said Annie.

"What exactly happens?"

"We walked out, closed the doors, there was a flash of light or something off of one of the windows in the second floor and then when we opened the door we were in their world."

"You saw this flash of light?"

"Sort of," said Annie. "It was kind of out of the corner of my eye more than anything. I've noticed the same thing when looking at the busy body mirrors when we go through with Mr. Ripa or Marcus."

"Interesting," said the President.

"Why?"

"Only those with our abilities can typically see such things. Even for our kind it often takes years to develop that ability. Of course, given your history you would likely have some level of ability, but to be able to see the flash with no training is quite impressive."

"Yeah, well whatever. But feel free to flash away, or do whatever it is you do so we can get there and get this sorted out and see what's going on."

"I'm afraid it's not as simple as that," said the President. "I've done what I can do and there was no flash, unless you saw it and I didn't."

"I saw nothing this time around. Let's take a look though. Maybe we flashed back and both missed the flash."

They opened the door and were still where they had been.

"Hmm," said the President. "Interesting. The portal let you and Mary go through unaccompanied did it not?"

"Yeah, but we had to give the bartender that coin first."

"We analyzed the coin and it was nothing but a token. There was no power in it."

"The bartender then must have done it."

"He would have had to have gone through the portal with you to open it. No. This was either you or Mary and I'm pretty sure it wasn't Mary. Come, we must repeat this again. Let's go back inside and come out once again only this time I want you believing with all of your heart and soul that we'll end up on the other side."

"Seriously?"

"It'll work," said the Council President. "You've got the ability to do this. Trust me on this. Let's try it."

Annie followed the president inside then tried to empty her head of all doubt and when she felt confident she flung open the door and marched through then closed it behind the President and looked up. A faint blue flash could be seen.

"Holy crap!" muttered Annie.

"You saw it again then?"

"Yeah," said Annie. "That was me?"

"It was. Let's see if it worked."

The President opened the door and led Annie into the bar on the other side of the portal. She walked to the front door and unlocked it and then stepped out onto the sidewalk with Annie trailing along behind her.

"Interesting," said the council President surveying the city. "I'm not sure I would have chosen the 1920's but it's not a bad time."

"I'm kind of a twenty first century girl myself," said Annie. "Did I really just bring us here?"

"You have no idea what you're capable of," said the President. "Believe in yourself and you can do just about anything."

"But I'm not like you."

"You have two eyes, two ears, one nose, you do only have one nose don't you? There's not another one hiding someplace?"

"No, no hidden noses."

"Then you're just like me. We're no different."

"There is that lock opening stuff you do."

"That's a learned skill that you could also learn. We all are the same and yet we're all different. That's what makes us human. Now, where is the last place you saw Wallace?"

"It was in the Mr. Lett's office. It's this way."

Annie led the way through the streets to the office of the old man. They only saw a few people on the street and those people didn't pay much attention to them.

"Here we are," said Annie pausing by the front door.

Annie nearly jumped out of her skin when the door opened and the middle aged Mr. Letts was standing there.

"Madam President. We've been expecting you. Come on in."

The oldest Letts was still sitting behind the desk when Annie and the President were shown in and seated before him.

"Madam President, It's so good of you to join us. I see you brought Annie with you. May I ask why?"

"I needed her help to cross your portal."

"Ah, so you've learned she can cross on her own? I was hoping she would discover that on her own, but so be it. What can I do for you?"

"My son and daughter are here. I wish to speak to them to be sure they're here of their own free will. Annie has assured me that Wallace stayed voluntarily after seeing what she believes to be his sister here. I need to know if that's true or not. I need to see my children. You know all too well the feelings of a parent towards their children."

"I can assure you that we would not keep them against their will. Even Annie's friend Mary would have been released had Annie been unable to comply with our request. Our threat to hold her here was little more than an empty threat to get Annie's cooperation. I shall have your children brought here to meet with you. If they choose to return with you to your world then they may do so."

He dispatched the middle aged Letts to find and return with the President's children.

"My sons were convinced that you'd show up with an army and declare war upon us, but I had more faith in you," said the elder Letts.

"Faith that was nearly misplaced," said the President. "It was Annie's counsel that convinced me that I needed to investigate matters before escalating things."

"Indeed, as I suspected it would" said the elder Letts. "Imagine that, a young descendent of the Letts who is a peacemaker between our sides. Wonders will never cease. Ah, they're coming."

Annie looked to the door and saw Wallace and Sarah enter holding hands and then the trio embraced as tears flowed down the cheeks of the President of the council.

"Are you okay?" she asked her children as she wiped tears from her eyes.

"We're fine," said Wallace. "Everything's okay. I'm sorry to leave you like that but once I saw Sarah I had to stay behind to see if she was okay."

"And are you?" asked the President turning to face her daughter who had tears streaming down her face.

"I'm so sorry for putting you through all of that," said Sarah. "I just thought this would be the easiest way."

"I thought you were dead!" said the President hugging her daughter once more. "You've no idea how good it is to see you alive!"

The reunion lasted for several more minutes before the elder Letts interrupted.

"Are either of you being held here against your will?"

"No," said Wallace. "I've been assured I can come and go as I wish. I was planning to return later today to tell you about Sarah."

"Indeed, something I encouraged to prevent this from escalating into a war," said the elder Letts. "We cannot afford to be at war with one another at this time. A bigger threat has emerged that may well require the best efforts of both of our communities to quell."

"A bigger threat?" asked Annie.

"Indeed," said the elder Letts. "I learned nearly a month ago that the beast was now stirring and would soon awaken. I've taken steps to monitor its activities and try to find a new way to contain it, but I fear my attempts at containment will fall short."

"The beast?" asked Annie. "What's the beast?"

"You would call it a dragon."

"A fire-breathing dragon?"

"Only in the real world the dragon breathes fire in, not out as your legends typically depict it. The beast absorbs energy and grows more powerful by doing so. The more energy it absorbs the more powerful it grows."

"But dragons are a myth."

"I wish it were a myth, but it's real," said the elder Letts, "and it's bigger and more powerful than ever before. Many people have died trying to contain it in the past and with our community now split, containing it once again will be nearly impossible."

"Are you sure the beast is truly stirring?" asked the Council President. "It's awakening so soon?"

"I'm afraid so, and it's grown to nearly double the size it was when it was last encountered. Containing it this time will be a real challenge."

"Why contain it and not kill it?" asked Annie.

"Because it cannot be killed," said the elder Letts. "If it could I would be only too happy to dispatch it, but creatures such as this are immortal. The more harm you try to inflict upon it, the stronger it grows."

"Seriously?" asked Annie.

"This is one of the many things our side protects your side from," said the council president. "The things of your nightmares are our reality. We use our powers to contain them. To send them to isolated worlds, which have been created to contain these types of beasts. In time though despite our best efforts they awaken and in some cases manage to escape their world and endanger ours.

"Creatures like this see no boundaries between the worlds and can move from one to another at the blink of an eye. They make portals, open and close them within seconds. Given free rein this beast will destroy all three of our worlds."

"Okay," said Annie. "Can someone tell me what exactly is the beast?"

"The best answer is it's a dragon, though that's far too simplistic," said the Council President. "It is one of many unique creatures that have survived for time immemorial and that will outlive us all. These creatures are said to have been created with the creation of the universe and they will ultimately consume it."

"They'll consume the universe?"

"Many have grown large enough to have their impact felt. You know them as black holes. They start out as smaller creatures though, initially no larger than a flea, but they consume power and energy. With everything they consume they grow larger and more powerful consuming more and more until eventually they've consumed all there is. They then consume one another until only one remains. Then that one will consume itself leaving nothing but the last speck of it which will contain all that was, and from this speck will then bloom a new universe and the cycle repeats."

"And they can't be killed?" asked Annie.

"Blows with a sword, arrows, or even bullets simply serve to toughen their hides. The deadliest poison only whets their appetites. Flames increase their strength. They can live underwater, between worlds and they've survived everything from the start of time until this day."

"But the military has better weapons now. Surely no monster could withstand missiles and high explosives."

"The Chinese developed gunpowder specifically to fight the beast and discovered it only accelerated its growth and made it more powerful."

"The Chinese fought the beast?"

"Have you seen the terracotta army? That army was created and imbued with magic to contain the beast. It held the beast in check for centuries. When it next awoke it took Merlin to contain it. He fought the best for five full days before finally summoning the power to contain it. After that it was up to the Green Witch who tried and failed to contain it on her own and then formed the Council who collectively fought the beast and ultimately subdued it. If it's now awakening again, then we must unite once more to contain the beast."

"So," said Annie. "What do we do?"

"I'd been hoping the answer to that was in the book you had," said the elder Letts. "The last time our kind faced the beast, the Green Witch led the charge and managed to subdue the beast and create the realm in which the beast has been trapped since that time. I was hoping some clue as to how she achieved that goal would be within the book, but there is nothing other than a narrative of her doing it and not how she did it."

"And before that it was Merlin who succeeded in containing the beast," said the President.

"Indeed," said the elder Letts. "Merlin's magic contained the beast for nearly eight hundred years before it broke free. I've reviewed Merlin's notes from the time, but they more tell me what doesn't work than what does. How he ultimately succeeded is a secret he took with him into death. I have however recently acquired Merlin's wand at great expense."

"The true wand?" asked the President.

"The true wand," said the elder Letts. "The British recently stumbled across an unmovable boulder while trying to build a road. Nothing they tried could move it or damage it. It was near Merlin's grave so I assumed he hid something of great value to him there and there is nothing Merlin valued more than his wand. Merlin had protected it well however. Nine good wizards fell and two others were damaged, but we ultimately penetrated Merlin's barriers and recovered the wand. I had hoped it would give us an advantage when we faced down the beast, but when I attempted to use it to quell the beast, there was no effect upon it."

"I have access to the Green Witch's Scepter," said the Council President. "If Merlin's wand fails, we have that to fall back upon."

"I fear we may need both and perhaps even more. The beast has grown in both size and power since it was last contained. I fear that we may be nearing the limits of our capabilities to contain it."

"How long until it's free?" asked Annie.

"It could be minutes, hours, or days, but I doubt it will be long. Reports from those monitoring the beast increased in frequency and then recently stopped completely. I fear they are no longer capable of reporting. That implies that it may be very close to breaking free if it hasn't already."

"How will you know when it's free?" asked Annie.

"It'll come hunting us," said the elder Letts. "The beast knows the danger our kind poses to it and it will seek us out first. It will attempt to pick us off in small numbers and weaken our strength. When it finishes with us, it'll move on to the mortals who pose no real threat to it."

"We must set a trap," said the council President. "Create a new world in which to trap the beast and use our presence to lure it there. If we place our collected populations there the beast will surely come for us. Combined we should be able to find a way to contain the beast there and prevent its escaping."

"It's a good plan, but we have very little time. The beast may even be breaking free while we speak."

"I can have my people ready within a few hours. Can you?"

"It should be doable, but we still need a place to send them. To construct a world takes days or weeks at best."

"We've got one already made," said the council President. "It's essentially an empty landscape with just two hills and a valley. We made it several years ago to serve as a training area for some of our kids. They can be a bit disruptive in a town setting. It's large enough to hold both of our populations and the beast. There is only one portal currently to it from our world, but Wallace knows its location and can create a portal from here to it also for your people to use."

"I can open a portal to the training grounds within an hour or two at most," said Wallace.

"Do it," said the elder Letts. "I fear time is our enemy. It will take all that both of our communities have to contain the beast once again. You must hurry and gather your people and I will gather ours. We'll meet in the training arena and wait for the beast to arrive. I dare say it won't be long."

"Let's go Annie," said the Council President. "We've got work to do."

Annie followed the Council President out and through the streets back to the portal where the President paused while Annie tried to clear her mind to open the portal, but clearing her mind with visions of a dragon on the loose was proving more difficult than anticipated.

"Can you do it?" asked the Council President.

"Yeah," said Annie. "I've just got to get better at clearing my mind. It's swimming a bit right now."

"Focus on the task at hand."

"That's easier said than done. Is all of that talk real? There's really a giant dragon about to break free and destroy everything?"

"Unless we can stop it and the first step in stopping it is to get back home."

Annie frowned and tried to force all thoughts but getting through the portal from her mind and then she saw the flash and breathed sigh of relief.

"It's open," said Annie. The two walked through the door and back into Annie's Philadelphia.

"Thank you, Annie. Head home now and take care of yourself."

"I kind of want to see this. Could I come along with you and the others?"

"Annie, this battle that's to come will come at a great cost. Many of our kind will die and if you're there there's nothing I can do to protect you. You don't have the experience to be able to assist us and honestly you'd just be in the way. This won't be pretty. It will be a war and there will be a price that has to be paid to subdue the beast."

"Okay," said Annie reluctantly. "I was just hoping there was something I could do to help. Sitting here not knowing what's happening will be tough."

"If we fail, you'll find out soon enough," said the President. "The beast will soon be among you and the world as you know it will end. If the beast does come through, try and find a safe place to hide. The subways might be your best bet. Life will be hard and likely impossible after a short time, but you never know what will happen. I've got to go now Annie, but it's been an absolute pleasure knowing you."

Annie watched as the President hurried through the streets back towards Elfreth's Alley. She walked back to her home and plopped down on the sofa while visions of a giant dragon consuming everything haunted her. She tried watching TV, playing video games, reading, and eating, but nothing served to distract her from the images of the dragon. She finally walked into her bedroom and collapsed on the bed. While lying there she noticed Mary's outfit lying in the chair where she'd left it after coming back. Without even thinking about it she was soon changing back into Mary's outfit. It disguised her once, it might just work a second time.

Chapter Fourteen

The entire Council had been briefed on the situation and word had quickly spread throughout the community. Within two hours of the President's return the entire community was gathered outside the Council building waiting for orders. The Council members finally emerged from the building and the last one out was the President of the Council carrying a large golden scepter.

"My friends," said the Council President. "Fate has once again called us to action. The beast has awakened and will soon be upon us. We need to confine the beast once more and we're planning to use the training arena to achieve just that. We've formed an alliance with the Letts and those under their command and together we will wait for the beast at the training arena and using our combined powers we should be able to once again subdue and contain the beast. I trust you've all made whatever preparations are necessary and are as ready for this as you can be. May fate be on our side. Now let's go forth and prepare to face the beast."

A portal opened in front of the Council building and the council members went through the portal one by one. When they'd gone through the rest of those in the area moved forward and went through. Towards the end of the line was a shabbily dressed young woman with a scarf covering her face, but no one noticed her as their thoughts were consumed with the task before them.

Annie listened as some of those around her muttered to each other.

"A bloody suicide mission if you want my opinion," said one old man.

"I don't know about that," said an older woman standing nearby. "I always suspected the old accounts were exaggerated to make those who performed the acts look better. With all of us and those of the other side combined, I find it hard to believe anything could survive."

"We'll find out soon enough," said the old guy. "I'm not sure I trust those on the other side to do their part."

"With the scepter of the Green Witch on our side I suspect we don't even need them."

"You could be right there," said the old man.

Slowly the line moved forward and finally Annie walked through the portal. She found herself in a valley between two grassy hillsides that sloped upwards a few hundred feet. Small shrubs lined the hillside and Annie ducked behind the shrubs to work her way to the top of the hill while the others all gathered in the bottom of the valley.

On the other side of the valley another portal was discharging the residents from the other Philadelphia. The two sides were near each other, but no real mingling was taking place as neither side seemed to trust the other. The elder Letts and his children were in conversation with the Council members when they all heard it. Annie felt the hairs on her arms rise at the sound.

It was a combination of a deep low guttural growl and a scream. The sound alone made Annie slide back further under cover as she scanned the skies for the source of the sound. The sky was a perfect blue with pure white clouds then against one of the clouds Annie could see a small black dot moving. The dot stopped moving and started to grow larger and larger and then the true scale of the beast made her gasp as it flew low over the crowd.

"Oh my, God!" muttered Annie. The beast was over a hundred yards long with a tail three times that length. Its head was the size of a city bus and its wings spread nearly from hilltop to hilltop.

The beast looped around the field and the two groups had now merged. Whatever concerns they'd had about one another had now been replaced with a new, more pressing concern. The Council President and the elder Letts were issuing orders and their followers were slowly moving into position to do battle. Annie looked at the relatively small knot of people and felt the situation was hopeless. Then in the midst of the knot of drably dressed witches and wizards she saw one brightly clothed young woman. It was Mary and she was wearing the new dress she'd picked out while shopping with Annie.

The beast finished circling and landed with a thud that shook the ground under Annie's feet. It landed a few hundred yards away from the group and then carefully folded its wings.

The size of the beast was enormous. Muscles rippled under its armored, scaly skin as it examined those challenging it. It seemed to have an amused look upon its face as it took in those arrayed against it. Apparently pleased with what it saw it now started to saunter forward towards the mass.

Soon, beams of energy could be seen shooting from the wands of the wizards including two larger beams coming from the scepter and Merlin's wand. The beast slowed slightly, shook as though a dog shaking off a fly and then raised its tail high and brought it down to Earth with a crashing thud. Annie lost her footing as did most of those assembled. Energy beams shot off in all directions for a few seconds as everyone regained their footing.

The beast now seemed to be smiling, almost laughing at those challenging it and Annie could see the fear on the faces of the people. They knew this wasn't working. They couldn't contain the beast.

She watched as the beast lifted its tail and twirled it in the air, seemingly unconcerned about the blasts still hitting it. The beast spun the tip of the tail into the crowd of people and sent most of them flying. Moans and screams of pain could be heard coming from those hit. Nearly all had been separated from their wands, so few beams were now hitting the beast. A few more flicks of his tail quickly knocked down those still resisting and sent their wands scattering. Its tail now encircled the group and slowly tightened, like a boa constrictor grasping its prey, forcing them closer and closer to the beast. Some attempted to climb over the tail, but the tip would send them crashing back inwards.

As Annie watched she realized that the beast was simply toying with them now. There was nothing they had left to offer in resistance. The beast was just taking his time and playing with those who had imprisoned it for so long before finishing the job. Annie turned away from the scene and couldn't watch until she heard a young woman's scream.

She turned and saw the beast reaching into the pile of massed wizards and witches and picking out one that caught its eye. The one it picked out was Mary in her bright dress. Mary was picked up and held by the beast as it examined her and then flicked its tongue out and tasted her. Mary's screams echoed through the valley.

"No, no, no!" muttered Annie. "Not Mary!"

The beast tossed Mary from one hand to another and kept flicking its tongue at her. He'd almost let her fall all the way to the ground and then snatch her out of the air. He was playing with her like a cat with a mouse as Mary screamed in terror. Fury raged within Annie at this abuse and she knew she had to act.

She had to do something, but what? It was then that she saw it. Near the right hind leg of the beast was a glint of gold. It was the Scepter of the Green Witch. She scrambled down the hillside towards the scepter then saw Merlin's wand also nearby. An image formed in her mind that was so clear that she knew immediately what she had to do.

She reached the bottom of the hill and ran across the valley to the foot of the beast and grabbed the Scepter and

Merlin's wand. Mary still dangled from the beast's paw as its tongue flicked over her, toying with her.

Annie quickly grabbed the two implements. She looked into the end of the scepter and saw a small golden cap covering the end of the scepter. She pulled on it trying to dislodge it, but it was stuck. In frustration she swung the scepter at a small nearby tree and with the impact the cap flew out. She jammed the gold covered bottom of Merlin's wand into the top of the Green witch's scepter and forced the two together. A bright golden glow emanated from the conjoined items. She then stood up and shouted at the beast.

"Put her down, or so help me God I'll use this on you!" screamed Annie at the top of her lungs.

Her voice was loudly amplified as it echoed off the walls of the valley and would have filled the largest stadium. The screams and cries of those trapped within the beast's tail quieted and the beast stopped tossing Mary in the air.

The beast turned and looked down at Annie. A broad smile now spread across its face. The beast let go of Mary and she fell in among the crowd contained within the beast's tail. Annie couldn't see her but prayed that someone or something had broken the fall and Mary was okay.

"Don't make me use this!" shouted Annie, but the beast ignored her words.

The upper body of the beast now turned towards her and the beast surveyed this loud little mortal. Annie waved the joined scepter and wand over her head and warned the beast off once more.

"If you want to stay awake then leave us! Don't make me use this!"

Annie thought she could see the beast smile at her threat and it swiped out with one enormous hand towards her. The claws on the hand were nearly three feet long by themselves and the hand was big enough to envelop a car.

Annie dove out of the way just as the massive paw reached her. The swipe did little more than plow up the soil where Annie had stood leaving deep furrows in the ground. Annie hurried back, out of the reach of the beast. The hand of the beast moved so fast it was nearly a blur, but Annie had been barely faster.

The beast looked towards Annie and reached out towards her once again, but Annie had now moved too far away for the beast to reach. She backed away still further and challenged the beast.

"If you want me then come and get me!"

The beast was trapped. In order to reach Annie it would have to move from its position which would release the prisoners.

The beast looked from Annie then back to those imprisoned in its tail a few times and then seemed to make up its mind. It started to slowly tighten the coil of its tail, crushing together the witches and wizards trapped within and producing fresh screams.

Annie realized what was happening and ran forward shouting, "Stop that! Stop that right this minute!"

The beast paused and looked towards Annie and then slowly continued to tighten the coils. Annie ran forward still farther and held the scepter and wand high. The golden glow from the scepter seemed to fill the valley with light.

"Don't make me stop you!"

The beast still did not stop so Annie pointed the scepter and wand combo at its head and prayed for something, anything to happen. A brilliant burst of gold energy shot forth from the device and struck the beast in the head. The energy seemed to bounce off the scales though and disappeared into the air.

"So much for that," muttered Annie.

Annie ran forward to get closer, hoping that narrowing the range would make the beam stronger, but

Annie's dash forward was apparently what the beast had desired as it now swept a hand towards her again. Annie had gotten too close and realized there was no retreat this time. The hand of the beast was but a blur as it rushed towards her.

In Annie's head a vision appeared of the tip of Merlin's wand penetrating the bare skin of the beast, but where was there bare skin on the beast? Protective scales seemed to cover everything but its eyes. She desperately looked for someplace to ram home the wand, but there was no place.

The beast swiped its paw towards her and Annie instinctively jumped up at the last possible second and somehow jumped over the paw as it passed beneath her. Annie looked to the scepter in amazement for the jump had to have been over twenty feet straight up, and yet she'd made it and landed with no harm.

"That's handy," muttered Annie to herself. "If I live through this I've got to get me one of these things."

The beast looked at its empty paw and bellowed with rage at having missed Annie again.

As the beast stared at its paw, Annie thought she saw exactly what she needed to see. The beast looked down towards Annie again and instead of swiping this time reached out very deliberately to grab her. He'd be ready if she jumped, ducked, or tied to run away this time. There was to be no escape.

"I'm warning you," screamed Annie at the top of her lungs. "Don't make me stop you!" She waved the conjoined wand/scepter over her head as she spoke. The glow from it filled the valley with its light.

Annie stared desperately at the paw as it slowly neared her and then she saw again what she needed to see. There was a small area of unprotected flesh, near where the thumb joined the rest of the hand of the beast. No scale protected that area. A small hint of pink skin could be seen with no scales or armor protecting it.

"I'm warning you one final time!" shouted Annie as her voice echoed through the valley. "Stop this now or I'll stop you!"

Annie stood poised and surprisingly calm as the paw closed in on her, finally the unprotected portion was within reach. She rammed home the tip of Merlin's wand into the unprotected skin and held on for dear life.

The wand and scepter glowed brightly and the paw of the beast froze in place before starting to shake so hard that it soon became a blur. Annie held onto the scepter and wand as though her very life depended on it. The shaking quickly spread throughout the beast until finally the entire beast was shaking violently. Then slowly the paw stopped shaking and became rigid and the rigidity spread from the paw to the lower arm, to the upper arm and then into the chest. The beast reared back its head and emitted a new scream, only this one combined frustration and terror at what was befalling it. Before the scream could end the head of the beast now also froze into immobility. The beast had been contained. The shaking stopped and the scepter/wand combination stopped glowing.

Annie pulled the scepter/wand combination free and backed away from the hand of the beast taking care not to get injured by the claw of the beast. She ran towards the front of the beast where the now paralyzed tail still encircled the group. Several of those imprisoned by the tail had now climbed atop it and were looking in awe at the beast.

"Is everyone okay?" asked Annie desperately.

"We're alive and that's saying something," said one of those now atop the rock-like tail. "Is it truly stopped?"

"I think so," said Annie. "I can't guarantee for how long, but it's stopped for now."

The Council president and elder Letts were among the first to emerge and be eased to the ground.

"I'd wondered why my sister had trusted the book to you," said the elder Letts. "I think we now have the answer. She must have foreseen this."

"How could anyone foresee this?" asked Annie.

"There are those who believe that all that will happen is decided in the moment of creation and we are nothing but actors playing out our roles. My sister was such a believer."

"How did you know to combine the wands?" asked the council President examining Annie and the now combined scepter and wand.

"I just got an image in my mind of what needed to be done and I saw the pieces so I did it. I had no idea if it would really work."

"The wand and scepter were made to go together," marveled the elder Letts as he examined it closely. The bottom of the wand was a perfect fit for the top of the scepter. "But how did you know?"

"Like I said, it just came to me in a vision. I could see the two combined somehow and knew that sticking the beast with it would stop it. I just had to find the right place and when it reached for me I could see a spot of bare skin and somehow knew to thrust it in there."

"It's a bloody miracle is what it is, but I'll take it," said the elder Letts.

"Is Mary okay?" asked Annie.

"She's a bit shaken up, as you can imagine, and her arm is broken, but she'll be fine," said the Council President. "They're tending to her now. You can see her in a few more minutes."

"When I saw the beast toying with her, something in me snapped. I had to do something to help her and that's when I saw the two wands. I knew I had to unite them and I did. So, what happens now?"

"We get everyone out and seal the portals using the best magic we have and pray that it's good enough to hold the beast for a long, long time. I'm glad you didn't listen to me when I told you not to come. We'd have all died without you."

"I don't know. I suspect someone else would have gotten the vision if I hadn't."

"Even if we had, there was nothing to do about it. We were trapped. We'd all be dead if not for you. We owe you a great debt."

"Just keep that thing out of my nightmares and we'll call it even."

Gathering everyone up and reuniting them with their wands took a while, then after walking around the beast a few times the portals were reopened and the people slowly trickled back through them to their worlds. Annie hung back, accepting congratulations and thanks until she was finally able to see Mary.

"Thank you so much!" said Mary who had her arm in a makeshift sling and a few cuts, but seemed otherwise fine.

"Are you okay?" asked Annie. "When I saw that beast toying with you, something in me snapped."

"I'm okay," said Mary. "If it's any help I'm no longer afraid of mortals. I've got a new monster to keep me up nights."

"I'm not sure any of us will forget that for a while. I was surprised to see you wearing the dress."

"Well, I wasn't sure I would get another chance to wear it. And if I did fall at least I'd look pretty falling. If we survived I figured there'd be a heck of a celebration afterwards and I wanted to look nice for that also."

"That makes sense," said Annie.

"Are you related to her?"

"Who?"

"The Green Witch. It's said she's descended from Merlin and that Merlin himself instructed her in how to contain the beast. I'm figuring since you got a similar vision you must be related to her too."

"I honestly don't know. Six days ago I knew nothing about any of this. It's been an interesting few days, but I have no idea who I'm related to. I can open portals and apparently contain mythical beasts, but I know pretty much nothing else. I just hope no future generation is counting on me telling them how to stop the beast, because I have nothing to add. If this hadn't worked, well, we'd all be dead."

"But it did work and you saved us all. Thanks again."

"Yeah, well, I couldn't let anything happen to you. We've still got to finish that shopping trip."

"I might need a few weeks for my arm to heal first."

"How does it feel?"

"It hurt a lot at first, but I'm feeling better now. We're fast healers and with good care I should be back up and around in a few weeks."

The party celebrating the defeat of the beast lasted long into the night. It was nearly four AM before Annie made her way back home and fell into bed.

Chapter Fifteen

"Annie! I'm back!" came the call from the living room door.

"God I missed you!" said Annie running out and embracing her mother.

Her mother looked around the unkempt living room and raised an eyebrow.

"I thought you said the house would be cleaner than when I left it."

"It's been kind of a crazy week," said Annie. "I fell a bit behind, but I'll catch up. How was your trip?"

"I loved the trip, but it turns out Dave and I may not be all that good of a fit. He's a nice enough guy and all of that, but being with him twenty four hours a day for a week kind of opened my eyes a bit. I'm afraid that relationship may be doomed."

"I'm sorry to hear that."

"So, what happened here?"

"The usual. The world was coming to an end but I managed to save it. By the way, that old guy came up with the money for the book and paid me for it. I split it fifty-fifty with the bookstore owner, so my college fund now has four million dollars in it. The other million is in a debit account for me to use on other stuff like clothes and whatnot."

"Yeah, right," said Annie's mother. "I'll believe that when I see it."

Annie pulled out the debit card and held it up while asking, "How about we go out to dinner tonight and it'll be my treat?"

"Where did you get that?"

"Like I said, the old guy paid for the book. There's nearly a million dollars left on this card. I did a bit of shopping with a new friend that ate some of it up, but there's way more than enough for a really good dinner."

"Are you serious?"

"Yes, I'm serious. It's been a pretty weird week. Oh, and I've now got a drivers' license. I don't know how to drive, but I've got a license."

"Did I hit my head or something coming through the door? None of this makes much sense."

"You haven't heard the weird parts yet," said Annie.

"It gets weirder?"

"A bit," said Annie with a smile

"How about we save the really weird parts until after dinner? Does that sound good to you? Where do you want to eat?"

"There's this inn I've found that has the best food you'll ever eat. A friend of mine works there. It's a bit of a trip to get there, but the food makes it all worthwhile."

"Is it a dressy place?"

"Far from it," said Annie. "They're a bit old fashioned, but the food is the best you'll ever eat. You should be advised though, that I'm something of a legend there."

Author's notes.

Thanks for reading this book. I hope you enjoyed it. If you did enjoy it, spread the word. Word of mouth is the best advertising a writer can hope to get.

You can follow me on Twitter @DonaldShinn or my blog at http://donaldashinn.blogspot.com/